Jonathan Hill is an auth  most significant work novel set in an English b g school in the 1930s, was named as the overall winner in the Self-Published and Small Press 2014 Book Awards. Covering a wide range of genres, he has penned the hit comedy series of *Maureen* books and the novellas *Pride* and *The Anniversary*. He has also published several collections of short stories and 100-word drabbles. He firmly believes that writing should not only entertain but also enhance and change the way readers view the world. When he's not writing and working as a pharmacist, he enjoys painting, photography and going to the theatre.

Kath Middleton began her writing with drabbles (100-word stories) and contributed a number to Jonathan Hill's second drabble collection. It wasn't long before she moved up a size to contribute short stories to anthologies. Shortly afterwards, she progressed to writing longer pieces and her first solo work, *Ravenfold*, was published to much acclaim. This was followed by the novella, *Message in a Bottle*. Her first novel, *Top Banana*, was published in March 2015. Kath likes to put her characters in difficult situations and watch them work their way out. She believes in the indomitable nature of the human spirit (and chickens). Kath is retired. She graduated in geology and has a certificate in archaeology. When she's in a hole, she doesn't stop digging.

Is it Her?

ISBN-10: 1530151058
ISBN-13: 978-1530151059

www.jhillwriter.com
www.kathmiddletonbooks.com

Is it Her?

Jonathan Hill

Kath Middleton

For Michael

Thanks for reading!

Jonathan Hill

Kath Middleton

Foreword

It all started when Jonathan was looking for some artwork for the walls of his apartment. While browsing, he came across Rod Buckingham, whose work he took to immediately. He sent the links to his friend and fellow author, Kath, and one piece, *Is it Her?*, stood out for her; she felt it told a story.

Jonathan and Kath decided they would each turn the image into a piece of creative writing. There was no collusion and they produced very different stories each written in their own unique styles.

The authors extend special thanks to the artist whose enigmatic painting graces the cover of this collaborative book. Rod has sold over 600 works, a mixture of busy Lowry-esque scenes and calmer, more contemplative pieces.

Is it Her? currently hangs in Jonathan's hallway, but now the authors are pleased to bring the painting alive in two moving novellas. They hope you enjoy reading them.

Is it Her?

by

Jonathan Hill

1

A NAKED BULB hangs above the card table. The light has been suspended there for as long as any of them can remember but tonight the wire seems dangerously thin and it is not difficult to imagine the bulb falling, its umbilical cord to the ceiling severed. And, normally cosy, tonight the small room is menacing and the shadows cast on all four walls could be the future ghosts of all four players. *Death*, they whisper, *is coming*.

One man throws down his hand. The cards spread across the table, feathers of a bird's wing. "I'm out," he says. His voice is deep, but lacks its usual strength. Tonight it falters, higher notes straining to escape.

"Then it's your turn for the kettle," the woman opposite says, with a smile that dissolves into nervous, rigid lips.

The man slides his chair back. It scrapes along the cold floor and hits the sideboard behind before it has fully cleared the table. The man slides out sideways, lighting a cigarette before he has reached his full height.

"She still controls you, I see," pipes up a second man, the forefinger of his left hand brushing his moustache up and down, up and down, up and down. He has barely stopped all evening.

The woman smiles then lets out a short, sharp laugh. The man with the cigarette holds it up like an extended finger. *This,* his action says. *This is one example of her not controlling me.*

"Well, it's true, sis," says the still-seated man,

his finger pausing horizontally just below his nose for a fraction of a second before making the short journey to his upper lip. And back again.

"There's no more beer?" asks the man who has risen.

No one answers.

The final side of the table comes alive briefly as the head of a third man lifts for a moment and then lowers again, eyes fixed on his cards, as if he's a marionette, strings slackened to return him to his default, slumped position. His cards appear smaller than the others' but it is the size of the hands that hold them which supplies this illusion.

"What?" asks - *challenges* - the smoker, outstretching his hand so the line of smoke from his cigarette deliberately wafts near the nostrils of Violet, his wife. She recoils, turning her face away as if it's just been slapped sideways.

"I didn't say anything," she says.

"There's no more beer?" he repeats.

"There's no more," Violet answers. Her voice is quiet, stuttering initially until it gains strength. "No more, Cliff. No more."

"No more," Cliff says. Then he repeats it, a question. "No more?" The glow from his cigarette dances around the kitchen, a firefly amongst the shadows. "There must be more. I know there's more."

"You've had enough," his wife says. "Tomorrow is a big day. You need your senses. You need to have everything about you."

"Tomorrow *is* a big day," Cliff snaps back. "Which is precisely why, my dear, I *need* more beer." He smiles to himself as he hears the unexpected rhyme he has just uttered.

"There is no more." This time the words are deep and come from the moustached man. The words of a man, even *this* man, reach Cliff's ears with more weight than Violet's and some part of Cliff's mind is tuned to listen to the baritone and accept. "Cliff, just fill the kettle."

But nevertheless he makes a show of resisting. "Excuse me?" says Cliff. "But who are you to tell me that there is no more of *my* beer in *my* house?" He jabs his cigarette towards the man's chest for emphasis,

4

stopping only when the cigarette points away from himself on the first 'my', attenuating - in his beery mind - the impact of his point.

"I'm Vi's brother," the man says coolly, his finger now lowered from the hair above his lip and curled into his fist, which trembles ever so slightly. "I'm the brother of your wife. If your wife says there's no more beer then so does her brother. Now fill the kettle."

Cliff sucks on his cigarette, exhales and paces. Sucks, exhales and paces. Sucks, exhales and paces. Then tosses it into the sink before spinning round and lunging for his brother-in-law.

Violet scrapes back her chair and stands.

"Hey, get your hands off Tom," she cries, her voice contained as if she's nervous of waking someone upstairs.

There is no one upstairs.

"They're not on him *yet*," Cliff snarls. But there is no yet, for Cliff's eyes have met those of the nameless, still seated man, eyes which echo his gently shaking head.

"Damn it," says Cliff.

"Never mind damn *it*," replies Tom, unfazed by the aborted attack from his brother-in-law. "Fill the *damn* kettle. My mouth's a desert here. It's all the damn smoke coming from over your way."

"It's not my fault the room's small," Cliff says, his voice almost a quiver. "I did say I'd smoke at the back door."

"You know that'd mean the rest of us would have to sit in darkness," says Violet.

Cliff grunts but hears himself sound like a frustrated cartoon character. He feels like a small sullen boy and colours a little.

"You know the light leaks out," scolds Violet. "We've tested it. You know that. And it brings in the flies."

Cliff snorts. "Yes, it's those pesky flies we need to bother about right now. Never mind the pesky Germans. And heaven help us if we encounter *German* flies."

"Are you filling the kettle or are you not filling the kettle? Am I, a guest in your house, going to have

6

to get up and fill the kettle?"

"Guests are *invited*. And *damn* the kettle!" yells Cliff. "There's a war going on. Men are dying. Right now, they are dying. And all you can talk of is the bloody kettle."

"Cliff!" says Violet. "We said we wouldn't talk of it. Not tonight. Please. And he *was* invited," she continues, laying her hand on her brother's sleeve. "I invited him."

Cliff ignores the latter words. "Because if we don't talk of it, then it doesn't exist? And if we don't mention Hitler, he isn't real? Really? Are we… are we six now?"

"Cliff, you know perfectly well that's not what I'm saying. That's not what any of us are saying."

"Then why not talk of it?"

"Because we've talked of nothing *but* it for months. Because we have a choice not to talk of it. Because tonight is our night. Because this house… this kitchen… *this* table is *ours* and not his. Because this time tomorrow you will be gone and Tom will be gone and all I will think about until you both return" - her voice breaks on the word - "is the war."

Violet's escalating voice suddenly stops but the words ring out and make the air vibrate horribly for several seconds.

All four are silent. One man is still standing. The others now sit, the only solid things in their lives the chairs beneath them. All are united in silence. Thirty seconds, then a minute passes. Then Cliff turns and picks up the kettle.

2

FOUR MUGS, half-filled, dot the table.

"We might as well be drinking hot water," Tom says.

A noise comes from the mouth of the man directly opposite. The nature of the noise is not clear. But given that the man has been quiet thus far, the fact that there is a noise is notable enough.

"Pardon?" says Tom.

"Hmm?" replies the man, if this can be called a reply.

"I asked you to repeat what you said, Jack."

The third man, the occupant of the quiet side of the table, the one whose hands make his cards look as if they belong in a doll's house, is Jack.

"I never said anything," Jack says, his voice crackling into life so it is as if Cliff, Tom and Violet are

9

tuning into him on the wireless.

"He didn't say anything," confirms Cliff, starting to reach over to Jack before changing his mind and aborting the move. In his head, he scolds himself.

Tom says something but it's mid-way through a swig of his drink and the words are lost, swallowed, drowned in his weak cocoa.

"Pardon?" Cliff returns the earlier question. He distorts his voice a little so it is closer in pitch and tone to Tom's. It is a thread's width from mimicry and it does not go unnoticed.

"I said that your brother has a voice," Tom says, his own voice rising. He jabs his finger diagonally across the table at Cliff. "God gave him a voice for a reason. And that reason was to use it. Jack here said something and I didn't catch what it was. I asked him to repeat it. That's all. I never even looked at you."

Violet's right hand comes down on the table, palm-first. Not hard enough to make a loud noise, but plainly enough to remind the others of her presence.

"I knew this was a bad idea. I shouldn't have -" she begins.

"You shouldn't have invited me?" Tom finishes.

"No, I wasn't going to say that. You're my brother and you're leaving tomorrow. Why wouldn't I invite you? I always intended for this to be casual, friendly. I mean, look at us... the rigidity of our bodies. Stiff... formal... it's as if we're cast in stone."

"Pompeii," Tom says.

"Sorry?"

"Like in Pompeii. Three men and one woman frozen for all eternity. Postures trapped and captured for future generations to gawp at. Three men and one woman." Tom stares across at Jack and repeats, "Three *men* and one woman."

Tom's voice changes almost imperceptibly on the word 'men' and Jack receives it like a bullet to his stomach, feeling ashamed and bitter towards the man who dares to speak to him, indirectly but not indirectly, in this way. He looks down at the discarded cards, wishing to render Tom as flat and lifeless as the

11

Jack of Hearts who stares resolutely, now and forever, to his right.

Cliff clenches his fists under the table, desperate to challenge Tom, desperate to topple him like a house of cards. But he fails to come up with anything that will not blow up into something much more unwanted and so he merely picks up from Violet's words. "It's not formality as such, more-"

"Yes, yes, I know," Violet interrupts. "Maybe we'll see Italy again one day…" Her voice fades out.

"I haven't been," Cliff says, after a moment wondering (and failing to see) precisely why the country is mentioned so suddenly.

"I know, but I have. With Tom when we were younger." *When going somewhere with a man - my brother - was uncomplicated and free.*

Words go unsaid and the air is still. Still but not quiet. Something hangs there, hovers. Something unseen. And it hums. The air is still but the atmosphere in the room is such that the vibrations of molecules themselves might be discernible.

The hum stops at the sound of a voice and, to

the surprise of all four, Jack included, the voice is Jack's.

"I *wanted* to fight. I always did. I *want* to fight."

The others look at him but, before making eye contact, turn away and look at each other. And something passes between each pair of eyes, a realisation, a sudden understanding of something not one of them had considered before. The fact that Jack might actually want to fight.

Cliff nods.

Violet stretches out her arm, lifting her palm from the table whence she half struck it not two minutes earlier. She places her hand on Jack's, almost gasping at how cold and bloodless it feels.

And Tom says something which leaves his mouth before he has even considered it. The words leave his mouth because it is natural for them to do so. It is his default. But even Tom himself sometimes wishes it weren't.

"What do you mean you want to fight? Nobody wants to fight. Cliff and I are fighting because we have to fight. I think I speak for us both when I say neither of us wants to fight." Tom is trembling again, but this time anger is the fuel. And the more he thinks how easy it is to defend your country in principle when you know you have a get-out, the more fuel that is poured onto the fire. "You've been told you can't fight on account of your leg. Just be thankful for that, Jack, and for God's sake, don't say things as stupid as you want to fight. Hmm?"

His head turns to face Cliff. Jack is off the hook, temporarily.

He repeats, "Hmm?" *As Jack's mouthpiece, what have you to say to that?*

Cliff shrugs and holds his hands out to ask what. Violet looks at them, almost shocked that they are both free of cigarettes. She notices that the tip of a nail on his right hand is coming away, half bitten. Two fingers of his left hand are stained yellow. Perhaps, she thinks, it is just the way the naked bulb is illuminating them and she wishes now that she could see his hands bare all the time and not holding a cigarette.

She'd considered her husband's habit many

times and tonight is no different. He'd always smoked but only on occasion. When Jack came to stay, occasional morphed into frequent and frequent became persistent. *Unrelenting.* There's no evidence of course, the logical part of her mind reasons, that Jack was the factor which directly led to a solidification of Cliff's habit, but her instinct, usually faultless, renders it hard for her to separate the two. Consequently, she has never fully warmed to Jack over the two months he's stayed with them since his work injury. And even when she placed her hand on his just now, she could not help but feel it was out of some vague duty.

She wonders if this will be the last time she sees her husband's hands in this way - open, clean, blood pumping through them - but she immediately shuts out the voice, not merely muffling but killing it.

"You made a noise," Tom clarifies to Cliff. "When I said that I speak for us both, you made a noise. As if to suggest you do not agree with me, perhaps?"

"Why is everything always an argument? I mean, tonight of all nights..." Violet says.

Tom holds up a hand to his sister while not breaking eye contact with Cliff. "You want to fight?"

It is not clear whether this is a challenge or a general question relating to the war. It isn't clear to any of those in the room but the person who has asked it. Tom is struck by the potential ambiguity of the question and he just about manages to halt a smile forming beneath his thick moustache. He is more than happy at this very moment to let the ambiguity hang there over the table like a thick pea-souper.

Cliff stares, his eyes boring into Tom's, Tom's boring into his, until neither man is aware that the black pits he looks into *are* eyes.

"You want to fight, Cliff? You want to go off and fight these... these Germans, huh?" He looks at Jack. *Or do you want to soil your underwear before you've left the house?*

For the first time, Violet feels acutely out of place in the kitchen, sensing its walls closing in on the table more than ever. She is well aware that the evening has descended, as she feared, into a battle of something else entirely... a war of masculinity.

Cliff blinks deliberately, severing the taut thread between him and Tom. He shrugs his answer. Tom grunts, picks up his cards, looks at them and then tosses them into the centre of the table.

"Cards never was my game," he says.

He picks up one of Cliff's cigarettes and scrapes his own chair back. Heads for the door which leads directly off the kitchen onto the side of the house.

"What are you doing?" asks Violet, sudden desperation in her voice. "The light."

"One more day won't matter," Tom says gruffly. "They bomb me tomorrow… they bomb me today. What's a day between us?"

"What are you going out there for anyway? It's not warm in here."

"What do you think I'm going out there for, Vi? I'm going for a smoke."

"But you *don't* smoke," Violet insists.

"I know," says Tom. "And don't worry. I'll close the door behind me so no *flies* come in." As he slams the door, he mutters, "Not that they'd want to."

3

TOM STANDS on the doorstep, cigarette in hand. A faint wisp of smoke, shrouded in darkness, rises skywards where it meets the hoot of an owl, an owl oblivious to all killing but the mouse it devoured for its dinner.

He thinks about Violet and he thinks about Cliff. But he does not think about Jack. To Tom, Jack is a coward, a pathetic excuse for a man, a mere sketch upon paper; he is the smoke that rises unseen from his lit cigarette, dissolving into nothingness higher up.

He does not think about Jack because he knows it will make him shake more. And in taking pains not to think about Jack, he ends up thinking of little else.

The door opens behind him and Tom does not turn, but instead steps to one side to allow Cliff to stand abreast, like a polite stranger at a bus stop. The owl hoots again as if to greet this new face.

Cliff strikes a match into his cupped hand then lights his own cigarette. He notices his hands are trembling, hopes that Tom hasn't seen but Tom has turned and is looking directly at him.

"Bit nippy," says Cliff, trying to explain away his tremor.

Tom turns again so both men are facing the black night the same way. He nods to no one and for no reason in particular. And Cliff nods too.

Two men nodding and neither knows why.

And the barn owl hoots a third time, the only being sure of its voice.

"The stars," whispers Tom, and Cliff is taken aback by the words, barely a breath. "Look at them," Tom says. "Look at them." He takes a suck of his cigarette, coughs and falls quiet again.

Then says, "We are blowing one another to bits and the stars just watch. Whether we live or die, kill one another... or love one another... the stars just watch. We shall extinguish one another," Tom says, "but no one shall extinguish the stars." He laughs, annoying Cliff and breaking the spell of his words. Cliff has never seen this side of Tom before and, to him, it is as if an actor has taken his brother-in-law's place and misremembered his lines. Only last month, Tom drowned a kitten in a weighted sack.

Tom shakes his head and tuts. The mask has slipped, the beer has taken him too far and he feels emasculated. *Does it matter?* he briefly wonders. *Out here, away from Violet and Jack, does it matter if I speak in this way?*

"And the night before we go, I'm speaking like... like a poet... like a damn *woman*. I blame the beer and this... this cigarette. Why... I mean, how can you smoke so much?"

Cliff shrugs. He hasn't always smoked so many cigarettes each day. *What changed?*

"I don't even enjoy it."

Tom laughs again but this time it's more forceful and he shakes his head in accompaniment.

"I don't," reiterates Cliff. "I suppose some part of me benefits otherwise I wouldn't keep on with it, but I don't *enjoy* it as such. Not like I enjoy a drink or a kiss -"

The owl hoots yet again, cutting Cliff off, but this time it is accompanied by a flurry of wings - the shaking of a paper bag - and it is gone. For now. For good? What does it matter?

"Or a kiss," he continues. "A kiss with dear, dear Vi."

"It's Vi I think about, you know," says Tom. "I mean, when we've gone, the Jerries can strike us both down, but it's Vi I worry about. It's Vi who keeps me awake at night."

Cliff nods, taken aback by the force with which Tom now talks of his sister, his words drenched in the sort of violent feelings that might accompany the contemplation of losing one's lover.

And then he stops nodding and a sudden anger rises in him. Anger at Tom and what he has just said and further rage at himself for accepting it without immediate question.

"Jack," utters Cliff. "*Jack.*"

"Jack?"

"*Jack*. My brother. Jack isn't leaving. He's here. He's staying with Vi. Jack can look after Vi."

Tom exhales deeply, tries to steady his hands. Words come to him but he dismisses each before it reaches his tongue and teeth and lips. Eventually, after seconds have passed - too many seconds - he just nods. A nod that is as empty to himself as it is to Cliff. And says, "Aye, Jack is here."

Cliff takes a deep drag of his cigarette, holds it in his mouth longer than usual then blows it out sideways, and for just a fraction of a second in his head, the smoke is a torrent of machine gun bullets.

Why is Jack always the afterthought, wonders Cliff. *Why is he always the afterthought when he shouldn't be?*

Jack is always an afterthought, Tom acknowledges, unaware that his mind is running on an adjacent track to Cliff's. *Jack is always an afterthought and he shouldn't be.* Tom knows Jack is dangerous - he has thought on this so often, *too* often - and he cannot quite put his finger on why he is dangerous or to whom he is dangerous. And every time he pursues the line of thought, through twisted, murky alleyways, he comes to the same terrifying conclusion. *Jack is a danger to us all*, he thinks. *He is a danger to us all.*

Tom loses his balance and he is suddenly a fish gasping for water in a dried-up lake. He falls backwards but the door stops him and he leans against it, unable to stop thoughts spreading through his mind like a ravaging disease. *If anyone should be putting their life at risk, it should be Jack. Weak, cowardly Jack.*

"Are you scared?" Tom asks, finally.

But Cliff cannot hear. His mind will not let it drop that Tom didn't even consider Jack would be here to look after Violet. A moment ago, he sensed Tom drifting backwards to lean against the door. He felt it happening in slow motion, as if in a dream. But he didn't turn. He could not bear to look at the man who cast aside Jack so ruthlessly, and then acknowledged that - *Aye* - Jack would be there, as if he were as much use to Violet as a broken teacup.

And so Cliff does not answer for he heard no

question asked. And as time passes, Tom, waiting for an answer, *needing* some sort of an answer, begins to think that maybe he didn't ask the question aloud at all.

Both men stand there in silence. Seconds and minutes tick by silently and eventually the quiet is broken when Tom whispers again, "The stars."

Only last month, Tom drowned a kitten in a weighted sack. And then went in directly for dinner.

4

"I THINK I just heard an owl."

Jack doesn't reply. He is just sitting and staring. His body has slipped into his former slump.

"Yes, I'm positive. It was an owl," Violet says, nodding to herself. "I haven't heard an owl for... well, it must be months. I thought they'd all gone. Gone to a safer place."

Violet sighs as she leans back into her chair.

"It was a silly idea. Not one of us enjoys playing cards!"

"It wasn't silly," says Jack. He is more willing to speak now it is just him and Violet. He has always been this way. In a group, he clams up and feels unable to say anything much, let alone express himself. But, for this reason, he fears times when he is with only one other as much as he is relieved. There is a real tendency for words and feelings, known only to him, to move from their steady simmering state and boil over, scalding everything in their path. It is now one of these such occasions, he and Vi together in the kitchen at this late hour, Cliff and Tom on the other side of the door out of earshot, when he is at risk of saying too much. And so he speaks every syllable in a measured way, much as a foreigner might when adapting to a new language.

"The point is not the cards," he says. "The point is that we are all here." He coughs to mask the breaking of his voice on the word 'all' but it is too late. It is not only noticed by Violet but it lances her in the chest and now she has an overwhelming urge to cry. No - not cry - *weep*.

"Do you think we will all sit round this table again?" Jack continues.

The question is met only with silence, and the owl sounding again. From the other side of the door, a deep husky laugh can be heard. It takes both Jack and Violet several seconds to realise it is Tom's. Violet cannot help but exhale briefly and sharply through her nose. She cannot recall when she last heard Tom laugh.

In her mind, the two of them are on a beach somewhere; they are small, just children, and he is laughing, squealing, a high-pitched yelp of joy, the sort that reflects inner peace. *But after that…* no, she cannot recall another time. There surely must have been times, she thinks, but they are not presenting themselves to her.

When she exhales through her mouth it is shaky. Each one of the words that follow - now she and Jack are alone, she finally has a chance to ask - vibrates with an urgency over which she has no control.

"What has Cliff said about me?" she asks.

The mention of Cliff's name hits Jack somewhere between his chest and his throat. It burns and he struggles to swallow before he can answer. But he can't answer. He is paralysed, a hundred thoughts swimming about in his panicked mind, a shoal of tormented fish about to be swallowed whole.

Violet has noticed his skin colour. It is white.

Pure white. And even his pallid features seem impossibly dark and bold against it, like black footprints against snow.

"I mean, he must speak to you, mustn't he? As a brother. What... I mean... what I'm trying to ask..." She looks nervously at the back door, aware the two men might reappear at any moment, their cigarettes burning out by the second, "... is whether he has said anything in relation to me when he goes to fight. He isn't the best person to communicate with. You know that. You've grown up with him your entire life, after all."

Jack swallows and it feels as if an entire apple is working its way down into the acid pit of his stomach.

Violet continues, aware that she is not giving Jack chance to answer, and unaware that she is offering a brief mercy to them both. "He doesn't speak much to me of his feelings. I suppose what I want to hear from you... and please don't tell me the words just because I want to hear them... they must be true... what I want to hear from you is that he will

28

miss me. That's all I want to hear."

Jack remains motionless in his slumped position. Acutely aware of the light bulb that hangs above the precise centre of the card table, he imagines it is illuminating nothing but his face. And it burns, along with Violet's stare.

"There is still tonight," he says eventually. "There is still time for words to be spoken." He does not look at Violet, but feels he must, if only he can bear to turn his head. To him, it weighs as much as a sack of bricks and his stare, both infinitely deep and shallow, only adds to the weight. Then he is suddenly struck by the realisation - an obvious one, and thus not a realisation at all - but nevertheless it still *strikes* him that he is sitting next to, not just Violet - *Vi* - but the wife of Cliff. And so he turns to her and looks deep into her eyes. Because he feels he owes it to her.

"He loves you dearly, Vi. He has told me so on many occasions. You have nothing to fear on that score." He takes her hand and holds it. It is cold but so is his and, together, they warm each other. "Nothing."

Violet nods, smiles and she allows her eyes to

fill, for now the right sort of tears are there, ready to fall to the card table, the floor, her lap, her breast.

It is true that Jack and Cliff have talked about Violet much.

And it is undoubtedly true that Cliff, when pushed, has spoken of his love for his wife.

When *pushed*, thinks Jack. Pushed by whom, *what*, Jack asks himself.

Tears make their own way to the fronts of Jack's eyes. He is powerless to stop them forming.

"I'm sorry," Violet says, seeing the tears. "I must seem awfully selfish. You must be on edge too. On edge something rotten. I've known him for so much less time than you have. It must be worse for you."

"He's my brother," says Jack. "My brother." And his tears fall for a reason of which Violet has no idea. If his tears were collected and mixed with Violet's own, they would separate like oil and water.

"There he goes," Violet says, sure she's heard the owl again. "Or she. I wonder if the call of a male owl differs from that of a female." It is put as a half-question to Jack but he doesn't answer. Neither knows nor cares. It is important to someone, something, somewhere in the world, but right now, in that kitchen, it is a grain of sand on a beach a million miles away.

5

"HERE THEY ARE," Violet says, trying to lighten the mood, for herself as much as anyone. "You look like two naughty boys coming in from school later than normal."

"Really, Vi," says Tom, closing the door behind him. It is a statement, not a question.

But Violet is determined that her faux spirit not be dampened. A switch has flicked in her mind and she feels it is now her responsibility to buoy everyone up.

"What's the temperature?" she asks.

"Of boiling water? Of the human body? At which ice melts?" replies Tom, without humour.

Violet can now no longer conjure up her brother's child self laughing at sand-filled sandwiches. "See, this is just how you used to be.

Tom, the brother who can't engage in a serious conversation for more than two minutes."

"If it's how I used to be, then of course it is how I am now. I haven't changed, Vi. Unless you think I have?"

Violet tuts then turns her chair fractionally away from her brother. "No, Tom, I don't think you have changed. And maybe that's the problem."

"The problem?"

Violet regrets her words instantly. But it is too late. They have already left her mouth and are dispersing throughout the room like a poisonous gas.

"I'm sorry, I shouldn't start on this now. It's not fair. It's not right. I always intended for this to be... a sort of celebration."

"Celebration?" Tom says, the word sounding as incongruous to him as it does foolish to Violet.

"Well, not a celebration exactly, given what... what is in store tomorrow. But... *actually*, Tom, this *is* a celebration. It's a celebration of the four of us. Let no one take that away from us. It's about man and wife. Brother and sister. Brother and brother. *Friends.* Is this not the point of living?"

Cliff and Jack listen quietly, look at each other and realise that each has been affected by Violet's impromptu speech. But Tom is still hung up on an earlier statement. He tries to let it go but the harder he tries, the tighter the knot turns. He is aware that his sister has just said something powerful - he can read this in the faces of Cliff and Jack - something that would no doubt resonate with him if he'd listened to and followed every word. But he needs to know what Violet was getting at earlier. He already knows but he needs to *know*.

"And maybe that's the problem," he parrots.

"Sorry?" Violet tenses.

"I want to know what the problem is, Vi."

The affectionate use of her name is deliberate, in that it isn't spoken with affection at all. Violet knows this and Tom sees that she knows this.

"Not now," Violet says.

"Not now? If not now, then when? When I'm in a field somewhere, my head a hundred feet from my body?"

Tom realises he has gone too far and he watches colour drain from all three faces. And when the colour is gone, he watches, helpless, as it bleeds from the room entirely. Until all that is left in his vision is the shadow of a table and three chairs, three ghostly almost-figures and a white bulb, screaming out its harsh light.

"I'm sorry," he says. Then louder, "I'm sorry."

Violet is shaking her head. Jack mentally makes his way to the toilet to expel his stomach contents. He sees the body on the field and the head a hundred feet away; the head is Cliff's.

"I just want us to speak plainly tonight," Tom continues, more softly. "Half our lives are spent saying things that aren't true or are deliberately cryptic... deceptive. If this... if this *is* our last night, then surely we owe each other the truth. Openness." But even as he speaks these words, he feels a fraud.

"Later," Violet pleads. "Later."

But the word pushes Tom a little closer to the edge.

"No, now."

"Not while the others are here," Violet says, almost a whisper as if trying not to let Cliff and Jack hear. Then she realises how ridiculous that notion is and she feels foolish, embarrassed.

"But we are close, are we not? You said yourself, not five minutes ago, that we are all friends." Tom now has no intention of letting Violet get away with it. "What did you want to say to me that you wanted to hide from our *friends*?"

The celebration, as Violet so determinedly put it, is falling away before their eyes. Her attempt at buoying up everyone has resulted only in her being drawn farther into a web so complex that no one thread can ever lead to the entire truth. Violet. Cliff. Tom. Jack. Each holds and withholds. Each knows and doesn't know. Each chooses what and what not to say. The picture can never be complete for any of them. *Never.*

Cliff recalls a bombed house in a neighbouring street, the remains nothing but lumps of rubble and, bizarrely, an intact lampshade. He stares across the table at his wife, imploring her to let it drop, yet knowing that when she and Tom start, there is no stopping until their own house is reduced to ruin.

"I was trying to spare your embarrassment, dear," Violet says, reeling from the tone with which her brother just referred to Cliff and Jack. "But as you are so intent on all being present… the problem to which I referred is you and the fact that you cannot keep a girl."

"Girl," Tom snarls.

"Woman then. *Lady* even. Who will you think of when you're out there? Who will be waiting for you on your return?"

"I had assumed, but perhaps this was terribly naive of me, that my sister might be waiting for me."

"I'll be waiting for Cliff. Cliff comes first. You must *know* that."

Tom shrugs. "Well, then Jack here will be the one waiting for me." He winks across the table at him.

Jack recoils in disgust, a red veil falling over his face.

How dare you make me feel like that, Jack thinks, tears springing to his eyes. *How dare you?*

"You see, you can never be serious," Violet snaps. "This is *precisely* what I was referring to just moments ago. Your tendency to reduce everything to jokes and smut. And the great irony is that you don't laugh or smile even. You never smile! And you wonder why on earth you are alone!"

"I wonder, do I? And how do you know that?"

"Please," Cliff pleads. "Not tonight." But the words are futile, pathetic. The night is already too advanced to be salvaged. Morning rushes on and outside the air is still; not a breath of wind to wash away what's being stirred up. In the morning, everything will be the same. It may feel different but nothing will have changed.

Cliff is roundly ignored, Tom and Violet locked in their own bubble, Jack still focusing on not being sick.

"Well, if you don't wonder," Violet continues, "the rest of us bloody do."

Tom stands, his chair skittering across the kitchen floor. The back door brings it to a stop.

"Where are you going?" asks Violet.

"I'm going home. Where do you think I'm going? Cliff, a cigarette please."

Cliff starts to extract one from the packet, but Violet leans across and holds his arm.

"No! You're not going anywhere and you don't smoke."

"Make that two, Cliff, if you will. I may well need another later."

Cliff feels the weight of his wife's hand on his arm. Tom is staring at him. His eyes are twitching and Cliff suddenly wonders if he will cry when he gets back inside his own house. Cliff hopes that he does, although he doesn't know why entirely.

Violet is staring at him across the table, the width of which seems to have shortened impossibly over the course of the evening. She is staring at him with an intense anger in her eyes. He looks down, realises that he has already handed over the two cigarettes.

A door slams and Tom is gone.

Violet rises from her chair. She should feel satisfied but doesn't, Tom's departure feeling as far from a victory as anything.

I just wanted us all together one final time. That's all, she thinks.

"I'm going to bed," she tells Cliff. "You two boys can stay up for a bit if you want. Turn off the light when you come."

She is leaving the kitchen when she turns back, walks over to Jack and presses her hand against his.

"When the others have gone tomorrow, you will stay, won't you?"

Jack almost laughs, the departure of Tom a great relief, something which has almost made him giddy. "Where else would I stay?!"

The reply is not sufficient for Violet.

"Of course," he says, knowing that Violet will need him as much as he will need her.

Violet is still standing there, her eyes glistening.

"Yes," he says. And then she is satisfied.

She nods and leaves. A minute later, the dull thud of a door closing above Cliff and Jack sounds.

Four are now two. More air to go around. But

it feels as if there is less than ever, lungs expanding and contracting with a tension that makes Cliff and Jack almost gasp in oxygen. The effect is the same to both men; terrifying, dizzying, thrilling even.

6

"MAY I turn off the light?" asks Cliff.

"You're ready to go to bed too?" replies Jack.

"No, we'll sit here a while longer, but I'd rather not feel like we're under interrogation!"

"It is rather like that," Jack agrees. "But won't it be odd the two of us sitting in total darkness? What if Vi were to come down?"

Cliff shrugs. "We can open the curtains. It's a full moon, or near enough." He stands, makes his way to the door leading onto the hall, cocks his head, listening. Then switches off the light, walks over to the window and pulls the curtains open, onto the stage that is the back yard at night.

He is just in time to see a black cat slink over the wall like liquid and land at the bottom. It walks about a little before settling in the corner next to a cracked and empty plant pot.

Not a care in the world, thinks Cliff. "Lucky devil."

"Hmm?"

"Nothing, Jack. Nothing."

Cliff returns to the table and both men sit in silence, a bluish light washing over their faces.

"It somehow feels more peaceful, more relaxing, with the light out, doesn't it?" says Jack. *Easier to speak,* he thinks.

Cliff nods in the semi-darkness, not wanting to intrude on the silence. But a few moments later, a noise sounds and it takes him several seconds to realise it is not the cat outside but Violet upstairs crying. He closes his eyes, willing it to stop.

Jack hears also and says, "Shouldn't you go up to see her?"

Cliff listens to the question, hears the words and repeats each in his head, over and over until the question makes no sense, until it does not even sound like language. And instead, he tries to block Violet out by speaking.

"The guilt became so much worse when we were called up."

Jack nods. "I know."

No, Cliff thinks. *You cannot possibly know. I am the only one in my exact position.* An anger boils up suddenly and he could quite happily punch Jack in the face. But the instant he thinks this, he mentally withdraws it and wants to apologise a thousand times and kiss him all over.

"It's the thought," Cliff continues, "the fear that I will not return and Violet will never know."

Jack, startled by what he's just heard, raises his voice: "What do you mean? We agreed she'd never find out. We promised. You promised me! If she were to find out then," - he pauses, delaying the words but then he decides to say them - "you might as well be lying in that field, your head God knows where!" The tears fall now. If Violet or Tom were still in the room, Jack would rush his oversized hands to his face and wipe them away ashamedly. But he lets them fall freely and Cliff sits motionless watching the ghostly blue rivers flow over his cheeks.

"You'll return, won't you?" Jack asks.

Cliff shakes his head, shrugs. "How can I possibly say? Either way, how can I *possibly* say?"

"If you die, then I shall kill myself. I *shall*. I shall kill myself!"

Cliff reaches out, grabs Jack's face by the cheeks and pulls him closer so their noses are separated by but an inch. His cheeks are cold and Cliff squeezes his fingers tighter, not thinking about whether he is causing Jack any pain. Tears are now falling from his own eyes. He uses his free hand to smear them across his face.

"You are not to kill yourself. *Ever.* Do you hear? You mustn't. Promise me you won't. Promise."

"Like you promised we'd never let Vi find out?"

"That's different," Cliff says, loosening his grip on Jack's face. Before he lets go fully, he strokes his left cheek and releases him carefully, like a fragile animal being let out back into the open.

"Do I tell Vi if… if you don't…?" Jack cannot bear to finish the sentence but Cliff knows its ending.

"You must say what you feel able to say. You must do what you feel up to doing. You are your own person. I can't make that decision for you."

"*N-No!*" stammers Jack. "I am not my own person. Without you… without you I am not *whole.*"

Cliff leans back in his chair, holds his head in his hands and screws his eyes closed. "No, you can't be saying that. You can't be saying things like that. Not before I go. Not the *night* before I leave."

"But it's true."

"I know it is," says Cliff. "I know it's true. But you can't be *saying* it. I can't… I just can't handle it… not when it's spoken aloud."

There is a pause and the ghosts of words float aimlessly around the small kitchen. Upstairs, Violet has stopped crying and drifted into a restless sleep.

"I feel guilt too," Jack says. "Having to say that we're brothers when we only met, what, five years ago -"

Cliff cuts in. "Five years? It's really been five years?" His eyes widen, amazed, as if he's just been told some unbelievable scientific fact.

"Yes, five years. Five years in September. Five years of thinking of nothing else, of *no one* else, but you, Cliff. Five years of saying our parents are dead when they're not. Surely it is a sin to mourn people who are still alive?!"

Cliff lets out an abrupt laugh. "And this isn't? *This* isn't a sin?!"

"You know what I mean, Cliff."

"No, I'm not sure I do. How can you be worried about sinning when you and I - *we* - are both going to Hell? And who's to say that our parents *are* alive? It's been so long since we were in contact. Out of the four of them, the chances are that at least one has gone. And while we're speaking of sinning, our parents - *both* sets - rejected us. They rejected us for who we were... *are*."

"I just wish," says Jack, "I just wish that we could be honest. I've been half terrified every waking second of the last five years that the people around us will figure out that we are not related. And even if they figure it out but don't know the *real* relationship between us, they'll soon work it out. Why on earth else would two men pretend to be brothers so they can spend so much time together, Cliff? I just wish - I *wish* - everyone around us knew about us. And once they know, they know and that's it. There's nothing else to fear." Jack takes a deep breath in and sighs until his lungs are almost painfully empty. "The thing I fear most is the thing I want most to happen."

"We cannot be honest, Jack. Ever. We are brothers. We are brothers until we die and then maybe there is a space in Hell for us to be more than that. You know... my dear, *dear* Jack, that this was the only way we could be together..."

Cliff stands suddenly and Jack feels his heart lurch. Cliff walks over to the kitchen door, opens it and stands in the hallway. He listens.

"What?" asks Jack. "What is it?"

"Hush! It's nothing."

"What have you heard?"

"I've heard nothing! I'm just making sure."

Cliff closes the door with a quiet click and returns to his chair.

"You know that the only way you could stay

in my life, and I in yours, was to make up that story. No, it's not been ideal and we couldn't be exactly how we wanted with each other but we were still close, weren't we? Brothers *are* close."

"Why are you speaking like that?" asks Jack, distressed.

"Like what?"

"In the past. We couldn't be how we wanted… we *were* still close… We *are* still close and when the war's over we *will* still be close."

There is a lengthy pause before Cliff replies, his voice breaking. "I know."

"Do you think Tom knows?"

Jack's question makes Cliff's head spin, both the change of topic and the harsh directness with which he asks it.

"What?! Tom? How on earth could Tom know? We've been careful. More than careful."

"I think he might know."

Cliff, panicked more than he'd like to admit, is suddenly desperate to shake the words out of his lover. "How? Why do you think that?"

Jack shrugs. "I have no particular reason. I just think it."

"You can't just *think* it."

"Maybe it's how he is around us. Maybe it's how he is around *me*. Did you see the wink he gave me?"

"Oh that meant nothing. He was being a fool. An utter fool. You're too sensitive."

"Maybe I am."

"You *are*," Cliff confirms. "But it's partly why I like you."

The hint of a smile spreads over Jack's face like a ripple then is gone, leaving the blue waters still. Moments later a frown appears. "What I don't understand is why you've gone to such lengths to be discreet and yet just a few minutes ago you said that you'd like Violet to know."

"Some day, I'd like her to know. It's most likely a dream but in an ideal world I'd like her to know who she's been with these last few years. The real me. If she were to find that out, then in my own mind - and this probably isn't logical - it'd be

50

somehow better. But as I said, that's in an ideal world, and this world is *far* from that."

"Do you think there will ever be a time and a place, not in our dreams, when *this* is all right?"

"I doubt it," says Cliff. "I doubt it."

Jack nods. "You know, I have a dream quite often." His eyes glaze over and Cliff sees him transported to another time, another place, in his dreams. "The sun is shining," Jack continues. "All day and all night it shines -"

"Well, that's not realistic for a start," interrupts Cliff.

"I said it was a dream! Let me finish, will you. Do you want to hear my dream?"

"No," Cliff says, laughing. "I'm joking. Carry on."

"All right. The sun is shining." Jack pauses, mischievously. "All day and all night it shines." He sees a smirk from Cliff and then carries on. "And we are walking through a park together. We're looking at the trees and you're pointing out a squirrel to me. We stand there for some time. It's probably a minute but it could be half the night. We stand there watching the squirrel. It runs this way and that. At one point it looks at us both and its eyes seem to laugh at us. We look at each other and laugh and then when we look back, the squirrel has gone.

"We continue to walk. And the entire time, the *entire* time, we are holding hands. Yours fits in mine with some room to spare, mine being large and all that. Not that you've ever pointed that out! You say that your hand feels safe, nestled in my own. But mine feels just as safe wrapped around yours. Then we turn a corner and there are people. People everywhere. Young couples, old couples, single people, dog-walkers and a juggler -"

"A *juggler*?!"

"I said it was a *dream*. Stop interrupting!"

"… a juggler," Jack continues, Cliff shaking his head in amusement, "and everyone is going about their own business. And we walk through them holding hands, and not one person turns to look at us. No one stops, no one stares. No one turns. And it is beautiful."

Cliff sighs shakily, suddenly choked with tears. For one moment, he was in that dream himself, for one moment, a moment he can only describe as beautiful.

A noise sounds outside and Jack leaps to his feet. The expression on his face is a picture to Cliff and Cliff cannot help but laugh.

Dearest Jack, he thinks. *I love you. And without you, I too am not whole.*

"Why do you laugh? There's someone out there!"

"It'll be the cat."

"*What* cat?!"

"The cat outside. I saw it earlier."

"Well you could have bloody told me!"

"I had other things on my mind."

"Other things indeed," says Jack, now laughing softly himself.

"Other things like us."

"Us," Jack repeats. "Us." It is then he decides it is his favourite word and he promises himself that it will be until the day he dies and beyond.

To others, 'us' is just a plain word. Two small letters making one small word. To Jack, however, it is the world.

"Violet will be waiting. I think my bed is calling," says Cliff. He stands and faces Jack. "I promise."

"You promise?"

"I promise I will return. I will come back for you. I promise."

The two men step forward at precisely the same time, their bodies synchronised like the second and minute hand of a wrist watch. And in that small kitchen, the blueness of a full moon faintly painting everything in its path, the two men hold each other. They do not talk. They do not kiss. They just hold each other.

7

THEY AGREE to go upstairs separately, Cliff first then Jack a few minutes after. On his way up the stairs, Cliff's mind is like a raging sea, thoughts and emotions hopelessly tossed about in a storm that offers him no chance to pin them down.

Violet is sleeping but he can tell she is ill at ease; the bedclothes are dishevelled, just like they are when she is running a fever. He walks round to his side of the bed and slowly and quietly removes his clothes, letting each item drip to the floor much like the cat he saw earlier. Down to his underwear, he slides into bed and gently eases the bedclothes over himself so as not to wake Violet.

He lies there, staring up at the ceiling. Closes his eyes tightly and sees an impossibly black sky peppered with stars. When he opens his eyes again, he sees that the stars are imprinted on the ceiling before winking out one by one. It is as if he's viewing an entire town from above and each household is turning its lights out in succession. He watches as homes chase each other across the ceiling to bed and the dark, dark night. A black-out. And eventually his eyes settle on two stars that remain in close proximity, bold, shining brightly, fiercely, resiliently. Cliff sees them as Jack and himself, defying the black-out, defying the world, but then the lights lose intensity and gradually dwindle to mere nothingness.

He hears the creak of a floorboard, can almost sense the vibrations from Jack's footsteps as he makes his own way to the adjacent room. He listens for the click of his door, wonders if he'll be able to hear Jack's own clothes gently thudding to the floor. And then he is aware of movement closer to him. He turns and Violet is staring at him, fish-like eyes wide, unblinking.

"Are you thinking about tomorrow?" she whispers.

"Yes," he replies, and then to try to convince

her, "what else?"

"You'll be all right," she says, her voice still hushed, conscious that Jack has just climbed the stairs to bed. "And we'll keep in touch by letter as often as we can."

Cliff nods but Violet does not see or sense this, so slight is the movement of his head. And so she just feels nothing, hears nothing.

"Cliff, there's something I want to say to you."

He swallows, wishes he were sleeping downstairs tonight.

"While you're away," she says - he feels her whispered breath on his cheek and smells something faintly sweet - "I promise to be here, waiting for you every day until your return."

Cliff tries to read into what she is saying, senses that there is something there, lurking behind the words.

"It's something that Marjorie said at the factory. She said it jokily but I'm not sure she was joking. She said that while her Steven was away, she'd have the pick of anyone left behind. I just want you to know that that would never cross my mind. Never. I could never do that to you and I don't know whether you've even considered this but I just want you to know that you're safe in that respect. I will never be unfaithful to you."

Cliff's breaths come a little more quickly and loudly. His eyes are screwed shut and he can feel a tear escaping. The words cut into him, burrow under his skin, and maim and scar in a way of which Violet has no idea.

"I know," he whispers. "I know." Then he turns and kisses her affectionately on the cheek, moist from her own tears.

A thud sounds from Jack's room. Violet turns her head to the door then turns back. Cliff is sure her body has tensed and he has the most awful feeling, which has been growing and growing over the seconds since her speech, that her whispered message of not being unfaithful was more pointed than it first appeared.

What are you thinking? he wonders. *What do you know?*

And next to him, separated only by an inch or two of wrinkled sheet, Violet waits for his tense body to relax after the noise from Jack's room, asks herself if it is normal to miss a brother more than a wife and lover. She imagines herself just for a second, prising apart his impenetrable skull and looking inside.

What are you thinking? she asks silently. *What are you thinking right now, this minute, this second?*

Violet's hand touches Cliff's leg. It rests there for several moments before inching higher. And then it rests there for another few moments. Cliff swallows, closes his eyes again and suddenly feels Jack's hand in place of Violet's.

There is a change next to Violet's hand and she senses this, receives it gratefully as a signal to continue. She moves closer and kisses him on his forehead, then his cheek, then his neck. She puts her arm round him, encouraging him to roll against her. He obliges, his eyes still tightly closed. When on top of her, he allows them to open, almost surprised that it is Violet under him, then closes them once more.

Cliff cannot help but feel that he has gone too

far but it is too late to reverse, and he is now inside her. Jack flitters across his mind, then Violet, then Jack. Two faces alternating rapidly at first, then slowing, slowing, slowing. He opens his eyes, unwilling to see whose face is in the final frame.

Violet moans softly, leans forward and whispers in his ear. "You never know, this may result in a little Cliff." *It must result in a little Cliff*, she thinks. *If the worst happens…*

They roll apart, breathing gradually returning to normal.

Violet wonders if this will ever happen again. Another stream of tears - the well, she is sure, is bottomless - leaks out and dampens her pillow.

Cliff wonders if Jack was listening, whether he could hear their movements and, if so, what he was thinking. The deeper he follows this train of thought, the greater the agony for him.

"I love you," Violet whispers.

"I love you too," he replies. But for the very first time, it strikes him that he is being unfaithful not to Violet but to Jack.

An hour later, Violet is asleep. Cliff has waited to be sure. Her breathing is steady, her sleep deep. He slides out of bed, feels the cool linoleum beneath his feet and stands there watching her for a minute. Walks round the bed to the door. Stands there for another minute, watches her. Her breathing is still steady, her sleep still deep.

And then he leaves the room.

8

JACK'S ROOM is square and small, and consequently easy to keep warm. Furniture is minimal. There is a bed, a small bedside table and a dresser with two functional drawers. (The third has collapsed in on itself.)

It is all Jack needs, though. He is grateful enough to have been welcomed into the house after his accident limited how much he could do to look after himself. Now, he's on the mend but has lasting leg damage and not a day goes by without him thinking that he could move back into his own home on the other side of London. But he hasn't mentioned this and neither has Cliff nor Violet. He often wonders if it's been spoken about behind their bedroom door. *Perhaps Cliff has persuaded Violet to let me stay?*

Sitting up in bed, he leans across and opens

the top drawer of his bedside table, takes out the folded leaf of paper and pencil. He knows it is time to do something he can put off no longer.

He rests the paper and pencil on his bedclothes and reaches back across to light his candle. While striking the match, his wrist catches his clock and it pirouettes before crashing to the floor.

"Damn it," he whispers, straining to hear if there is any movement from the adjacent bedroom. *Nothing.*

Then he lights the candle and tilts his paper towards it. As he writes, leaning against his knees, the pencil pushes through leaving a tiny bullet-hole shape. "Damn it," he whispers again, turning the paper over and smoothing it out before continuing to write with less pressure.

The words flow fairly easily and he wonders why he has delayed his writing of the letter for so long. His brain is tired and logic dictates that he should be finding it difficult, emotionally exhausting. But the words come to him with a welcome, unexpected ease. This, he reasons, is because it is not his hand moving the pencil but his heart.

He stops just once, looking up to recall how he and Cliff first met. And he remembers it now exactly as it happened, as if he is experiencing it for the very first time tonight.

It is cool but sunny and the patches of warmth, when I'm out of the shade, are deliciously comforting. It's what I need. Comfort.

Summer is on its way out but there are still people everywhere, enjoying the sunshine. I haven't planned to stop anywhere but at the very last second, somewhat inexplicably, I turn into Bloomsbury Square. It is fairly busy, as is to be expected, but immediately a corner of the square stands out. A lone man occupies a bench and he is surrounded by a halo of space.

I walk over, admiring the plants, but taking furtive looks at the man every so often. He doesn't look up once, for he is engrossed in a book. I cannot see his face properly yet I am drawn to this man, a moth to a flame.

When I reach the bench, I cough gently. The man looks up from his book and something changes in his eyes.

We look at one another for a second or two and then I dare to ask, 'Is anyone sitting here?'

'Yes,' the man replies.

My heart collapses in on itself a little and I simply nod.

'Me,' the man says. 'I'm sitting here.' He is smiling, clearly enjoying pulling my leg.

'I see,' I say, a little frustrated with him, but secretly delighted that this man feels comfortable enough to be this way with me.

'There's no one else planning to sit here, then?' I ask.

'Yes,' the man says, smirking again.

I look around but there is only me anywhere near the bench.

'You,' the man clarifies. 'You're planning to sit here.'

I smile, check the wooden planks for bird droppings - for my trousers are clean on today - and sit down at the opposite end of the bench.

'I don't bite,' the man says. His eyes are warm and kind and nothing else matters. Everything I want and need *is in those eyes.*

'I know,' I say. 'But you're reading. Don't let me disturb you.'

The man shakes his head and laughs, as if he thinks I am a curiosity. Well, I suppose I am.

I sit there, inhaling and exhaling in a measured way. I smell the greenery, watch a squirrel darting about, nod at a passing couple and, every now and again, sneak a look at the man with whom I share the bench.

After several minutes, the man snaps his book closed with a tut.

'It's no good,' he says. 'I can't concentrate.'

I look at him, shocked at his abruptness and apparent temper.

'Not with a good-looking chap like you sitting there.'

My heart melts and I am barely able to speak.

'How... h-how do you know?' I stutter.

The man shrugs, 'It's a sort of sense, I suppose. You have to have this sense to get anywhere if you're like we are.'

I look at him, amazed.

He extends his hand to me. 'Cliff,' he says.
I nod, smile. 'Jack,' I say. 'My name's Jack.'

When the letter is done, Jack reads it over, then holds it to his chest. Feels his heart beating strongly against the fragile paper.

When the door creaks open, he thrusts the letter under his pillow and turns, alarmed.

"Cliff?" he says. "What are you doing?"

Cliff puts his finger to his lips, pushes the door closed and pads over to his bed.

"Are you going to lie there, or move over and let me in?"

"Sorry," says Jack. "I wasn't expecting you, that's all."

"No," replies Cliff, "neither was I!"

Both men lie still, staring up at the ceiling. The sides of their bodies are touching. Their legs exchange warmth.

"Cliff?" Jack asks, for Cliff is crying. "Cliff?"

"Hold me," Cliff says. "Hold me."

And Jack holds him.

They lie there in that pose for a long time, holding each other. Cliff would be quite happy if it lasted the entire night. *And maybe,* he thinks, *it would be best if Hitler sent a bomb crashing through the window this very second, so that we can both die in this embrace.*

Every now and again, their hands explore a little farther from where they hold each other, but they do not stray far before returning their bodies to their tight embrace.

There is no need for words. They have spent the best part of five years talking. They have talked themselves out. Now they need just each other's contact. The final piece to the jigsaw.

Not a minute passes between each instance when they turn to look at each other. In the soft candlelight they can make out each other's smiles. Smiles tainted with sadness, regret, a too-solid sense of everything coming together much, much too late.

And sometimes they kiss each other. On their foreheads, on their cheeks, on their lips.

It is during one such kiss - alas, on the lips - when the door creaks open again and they turn to see

Violet standing there, her arms hanging by her side like dead weights.

She stumbles backwards and the wall breaks her fall. Then she goes crashing forward onto the bed, pummelling the pair of them, screaming at them. She wants an explanation. She wants to know what brothers are doing together in bed kissing, not out of fraternal affection, but on the lips. She wants to know why on earth they think they can get away with this under her roof. And most of all she wants to punish herself for not listening to her earlier doubts, her instincts that something was not quite sound; the introduction to Cliff's brother a little too late on in their relationship, the too frequent disappearances of Cliff from their bed at an ungodly hour, the too eager pleading from her husband to allow Jack to stay with them after his accident.

Too, she thinks, *is a word I despise. It's a word that has always been there, hovering like a disease-ridden mosquito, and it let me wait, let me suffer and now it has bitten, ironically, too late.*

Her fist catches Jack in the eye, her other

strikes Cliff's cheek. The three of them tumble around on the bed until Violet loses her balance - although to her it feels more like a brief loss of consciousness - and falls to the floor.

Cliff pounces on top of her and holds her wrists to the floor, sits astride her legs to stop her thrashing about.

"Listen," he says, breathlessly. "Listen, there's something you need to know." His heart is racing like a driverless locomotive train.

Violet shakes her head. "No, no, *no!*" she screams over and over.

Jack looks down from the bed at them, helpless. To him, it looks like a scene that might happen during childbirth or a violent rape.

"No, no, *no!*" Violet screams.

The neighbours are the last thing on her mind, but Cliff panics that alarm will be raised and he lifts his hand, holds it suspended for a moment, then strikes her cheek. If her hand were free, she'd whip it there and hold herself, stunned, but as she is, she can only watch, horrified. *You - you're a monster.*

"Listen, Violet, listen! Jack isn't my brother. He's a friend. He's a very good friend and he's just consoling me. That's all."

"No, I saw. I *saw*!" Violet wails. "Get him out! Get him out! Get him *out*!"

"I'm going," Jack says, eyes flashing about the room. The candle flame, miraculously still alight, is thrashing about from side to side, whipping the air. At one point it is almost extinguished but then springs up again with renewed energy.

"No," roars Cliff.

"Yes," Jack says. "Half the street will wonder if someone's being murdered. I have to go. I have to go now."

"No, please, stay," begs Cliff, Violet no longer in his vision. In his head, he is looking up at the ceiling again at a pair of stars and their light is faltering, and he is terrified.

Violet sees her chance, feeling the pressure on her limbs weaken. She uses all her strength to tip Cliff off her, scrambles to her feet and lunges at Jack, tears clouding her vision.

"Why?" she asks him, pummelling Jack's chest. But she has no fight left and her hands weakly flail about. *"Why?"*

"I'm sorry, Vi. I truly am. I'm going. I'll get my things together and then leave."

"No," says Violet.

Jack stops. *Has she changed her mind suddenly?*

"Leave your things. Get out of my house. Get out. *Now!*"

"Let me at least get dressed, then."

Violet steps aside, allows him to pick up his clothes, stands facing the wall, her back to him - a charade of polite stiff-upper-lip Britishness, the ridiculousness of which she is oblivious to - as he dresses himself.

Even while her back is turned, Jack cannot bear to look into Cliff's eyes, but he does so briefly, as he thrusts the letter from under the pillow into his hand.

Moments later, the front door closes and Cliff and Violet are left alone, standing but, inside, on their knees. Now, to both, the battlefield is the most welcome place on Earth.

9

HE'D EXPECTED so much to have changed but it hasn't. Not near his former home anyway. The streets, the houses, the pillar box on the corner all greet him like old friends. He feels that there is something reassuringly comforting about this but at the same time it is not what he wants. He's come back but not to stay. He is on the receiving end of odd looks from those who are braving the weather on foot, for he is driving so slowly. *Well,* he thinks, *there is no one behind me. I am not hindering anyone.*

He'd expected to feel so much more than he does at present. But the tiredness, so persistent and long-lasting it too feels like an old friend, clouds everything.

He is nearing his old street when he sees her. At least, he thinks it's her. He cannot be sure and he drives past initially, then brakes a little further on. Takes a deep breath then swings open his door and gets out.

He turns and stands there, the rain lashing down, mini rivers flowing down the channels created by his long coat. She is dressed all in red, holding a matching umbrella. *It cannot be her. She never dressed in this way. She hated to be the centre of attention. Violet would not wear this colour.*

A man, walking his dogs, stops, the sight striking him as odd and he feels that the world has stopped turning. He holds his breath, not understanding why. He senses that what he is watching unfold - not that anything *is* unfolding, at least not yet - is significant, momentous even. He nervously moves his thumb in a circular motion over the side of his forefinger. Over and over. His fingers, stained with all the colours of the rainbow, are cold, but he forgets this and mentally captures the scene before his eyes. A scene he will recreate on canvas that very same day. He can already sense the brushes in his hand; they warm his fingers.

Cliff takes a step away from the car.

The spell is broken for the painter and, as he watches Cliff walking slowly through the driving rain, he turns to leave. His artistic mind is satisfied with the enigmatic scene and he does not wish to see any more.

"Come on, Rod," he says, with a whistle.

Rod is nosing about at the bottom of a drainpipe of a nearby house. The water is gushing down and tickling his face. He is having enormous fun but his master has called him, and so he must go.

The painter, walking away, whistles again and Rod goes bounding after him.

Cliff coughs as he approaches her. She does not turn at first and he thinks that maybe she has seen him and is ignoring him, hoping he will get back inside his car and drive off.

He coughs again and as he lifts his fist to do so, water pours down his sleeve. She turns gracefully, tilting her umbrella to reveal her face.

"Violet?"

"Cliff," she says. "Cliff."

The pair are unsure whether to step forward a little closer to each other, but they decide to stand where they are, Violet sheltered, Cliff in the rain.

"I didn't expect to see you again," she says, tears pricking her eyes. "You look... you look..."

"Different?" Cliff asks.

"Well, no... you look... well, you look just the same." Violet hates herself for saying this aloud for it confirms to her just what she is thinking. She never intended to see Cliff again and, if she did, she always imagined him to look wildly different, changed by the war, and this, she had convinced herself time and time again, would have made the encounter so much easier to deal with.

And just as Violet never intended to see him again, Cliff never intended to return to this street. But after standing on Jack's doorstep for some time, no answer to his knocks and shouts, he has nowhere else *to* go. He wants desperately to ask Violet about his lover, but he thinks it rude so early on in their meeting and he has no idea how she will react. Furthermore, he expects she will have as much idea about where

Jack is as Cliff himself does.

"*You* look different," he tells Violet, looking her up and down. "Red," he says, "it makes you look so much more… well, confident, I suppose."

She shrugs. "Thank you."

He wants to ask her why she never wore red while they were together but doesn't.

"Are you well?" he asks.

"Yes. Thank you." She pauses. "You?"

"As well as I can be," he says. *As well as I can be after what I've been through.*

He cannot hold it in any longer and the question erupts out of him.

"Have you heard anything from Jack?" *He answered, without fail, on the very first knock every time I had leave.*

Violet turns away. She had been expecting this and is only surprised it took him this long to ask.

"Violet?" he asks. "Vi?" *Without fail.*

She turns. "It's Violet. And I assumed you'd already heard?"

"Heard?" *The very first knock.*

"About Jack."

"What about Jack?" He is hearing the conversation unfold dully, the rain at the fore. He feels he is watching the pair talking. He doesn't feel *one* of the pair.

"Jack's not here any more," she says.

Cliff does not understand. Will not allow himself to understand.

"He's moved away? Why?"

Why would he move away? I saw him just weeks ago. What's changed? It's over now. The whole thing is over and now I can be with him forever and ever and ever. I will never have to leave him again.

"No," Violet says. "He's no longer... he *died*."

A spontaneous whimpering sound tumbles from Cliff's mouth. He recalls the last time they parted, Jack's usually strong embrace something much more fragile and, he thinks now, perhaps devoid of hope.

He killed himself, Cliff thinks. *The stupid, stupid...*

The thought is extinguished as if Violet is

reading his mind. "He was helping out after a raid. A building collapsed. At least that's what I heard."

"At least that's what you heard?"

"I found out from a friend. Well, a friend of a friend." She pauses, bites her lip. "I'm sorry," she adds.

Cliff nods, is aware of nothing else except the fact that he is nodding. He wants to leave.

And he turns without even saying goodbye. But then, just as sharply, turns back.

"And Tom?"

"Tom?" she asks, pronouncing the name as if they don't know and have never known a Tom. She bites her lip again, her heart pounding against the fabric beneath her coat. She hears Tom's voice, his stern words, sees his face. She gives Cliff a little shake of the head.

Cliff nods in reply.

Dead.

Both dead.

In his mind, the information is dull, incomprehensible, and liquid, as if it might reform and reshape into something entirely different before it solidifies. But Jack is dead. He will not un-die. And this, in time, will hit Cliff with a force a million times greater than an exploding grenade.

He turns silently to leave but, two paces away, he stops at Violet's voice, turns round again to face her.

"Cliff?" she says.

Two images fill her mind; the pair of them laughing together at something she has forgotten, and the sight of another letter from Cliff plopping through her letterbox, another letter she'd open, read and not answer. She has occasionally felt guilt at not replying to Cliff's letters, not acknowledging in any way the confused apologies from his tortured soul. But she'd never been able to bring herself to reply, because to do that would be to acknowledge his relationship with Jack.

But now Cliff is in front of her again and, physically - miraculously, she thinks - he is not much different from before. But something has changed between them, a barrier has eroded over time, a veil lifted, and she is certain that she can see beyond his skin, and what she sees compels her to say words which she'd never dreamed she'd utter to him.

"Cliff?" she hears herself say. "Find someone else and be happy."

Cliff stares at her, realising he will have to process this later.

And now it is Violet who walks off first, leaving Cliff to make the short journey back to his car.

He is reaching out for the door when the hit comes. He collapses and falls to his knees. Tears are streaming down his face, merging seamlessly with the rain. To Cliff, the world is one big river and he just wants to be washed out to sea.

He opens his mouth. Tries to say something. Closes it.

He has three more attempts, all unsuccessful.

Then he manages it. The word comes out in a choking splutter and Cliff finds it agonising to hear it come from between his lips.

"Jack."

10

CLIFF MINDS THE GAP as all three legs - his stick included - board the Underground train. He shuffles down the carriage and squeezes in between a very young-looking pregnant woman, Madonna's *Like a Virgin* leaking out from the headphones of her Walkman, and a young man with a hairstyle he thinks looks ridiculous.

Whatever next? What is wrong with these people?

Then he reflects and comes to a realisation.

What is wrong with me? Perhaps it is not others who are wrong...

What is wrong with me? he thinks.

I am old.

That is what is wrong.

Twenty minutes later, just before the train pulls into the Russell Square station, he struggles to his feet. The pregnant woman supports his back as he stands.

"Thank you," Cliff says, lifting his stick a little as a gesture of thanks.

Outside, he looks up and down the road, deciding on the direction he needs to take. He has come alone. He has convinced himself that this is something he can only do alone.

He hasn't been here for a long time.

So so long, he thinks.

The sun is out and it feels pleasing on his leathery face. The traffic, both off and on the pavement, is heavy and it takes him a good while to reach his destination safely. He pauses briefly next to a restaurant on Southampton Row - it wasn't a restaurant back then, of course, but it is this spot where he saw Tom several years after his final meeting with Violet. Tears had sprung to his eyes at the thought that Violet had lied to him. He'd replayed the scene in the rain so many times, though, that his changing memory of it had distorted the truth. At the time, Violet had merely shaken her head. She had not, contrary to Cliff's later recollection, uttered the words that Tom had died.

He had misread her.

Since the sighting, Cliff had thought and thought about why he'd been led to believe that Tom was dead. He had concluded that Tom had ordered Violet to make out as if he'd died. Perhaps, Cliff supposed, that would have made it easier for Tom, not having to confront the man who'd betrayed his sister.

Tom hadn't seen Cliff that day. Cliff had made sure of that.

He stands now outside the square for several minutes, conjuring up the inner strength he needs. While there, he is asked to pose for a Japanese photographer - *Is it the world that is mad or is it I who need to be led away in a straightjacket?* - and is requested to show a family of four how to find a place of which he has never heard.

Eventually, he slopes into Bloomsbury Square. The bench is still there. It is not the same bench, of course. It is more modern. But its position is the same

- remarkably, Cliff thinks. And it is empty. Despite the weather, there are only several others dotted about, exposing their pale skin to the sun's rays. The bench is empty as if expecting him.

He makes his way over to the bench, sits down on one end and rests his stick against the litter bin alongside. A child runs past, screaming, an empty ice-cream cone in her hand. In the other direction runs a grey squirrel. It stops not two feet from Cliff's shoes and looks him in the eyes. Cliff cannot help but smile and, when the squirrel has finally run off, he turns to find a man sitting on the other end of the bench.

How did I not see him sit down?

Cliff answers away his own question, considering it a failing of his peripheral vision. But he isn't certain.

The man smiles, amused also at how the squirrel took a shine to Cliff. He nods and Cliff, slowly and after a delay, as if he is in a dream, returns the nod. And then the man pulls out a book, turns to a page somewhere in the middle, unfolds the page's corner, smooths the crease, and begins to read. Cliff focuses for a moment on the hands holding the book. They are what Cliff would call normal hands. Not too small and certainly not too big, he thinks.

Cliff reaches into his own pocket and pulls out his wallet. Its leather is shabby and the wallet in need of replacing but Cliff thinks it is probably not worth it. Out of the wallet, he extracts a piece of paper, folded twice.

The paper is in poor condition. Three of the four corners are torn. Not one inch of the surface is free from smears of dirt. There is a hole in the page, small, made by a pencil, near the top left corner. And the words? Several are visible here and there. Most have been worn away by time itself. But Cliff can fill in the gaps. He knows the letter by heart but he wishes to hold it here, in Bloomsbury Square, as he 'reads' it.

With his free hand, he wipes his eyes, then focuses on the letter.

My dear dear Cliff,
Firstly I should apologise for the hole in the paper.

It's my fault for trying to write on the bedding. For once, though, it wasn't due to my stupidly large hands(!)

It's not easy for me to give you something to remember me by for obvious reasons so I thought I'd write a few words. They'll be something you can keep close at all times, wherever in the world you are. You do know I'd come with you every step of the way if I could, don't you?

I don't want this to sound like a goodbye letter. It isn't and I will wait for you until your return. I shall not move! However, there are things I have to say just in case.

My life changed when I first met you that September day in Bloomsbury Square. I can't say precisely how, other than that you filled the hole in my soul. For that I need to thank you and I can only hope I have given you something in return. If not, then maybe I can make up for it when you come home to me.

Did you notice how I put that? I wrote 'when'. Let's keep positive, Cliff. There are enough of you going out there to win this war. That's surely a good sign. Strength in numbers and all that.

I promise to look after Vi while you're away. She has been ever so kind in letting me stay with you both. I will keep her safe.

Remember that I am thinking of you at all times. No matter how hard it is for you out there, I am with you. Remember that. And remember my dream. One day, in this world or the next, we will be walking hand in hand and no one will care one jot.

Much love always
Jack

Cliff looks up, his eyes glazed over, frozen lakes about to melt. And he nods. Over and over, he nods, until his body gently shakes.

Clusters of people walk by. One woman steers her child away from him. *Stay away from the mad man,* she communicates to the young boy with a tilt of her head.

Cliff is breathing heavily. In and out. In and out. In and out. His eyes are closed and he feels something happening. He feels something changing. He can feel its warmth spreading throughout his body from head to toe, inside to out. And when he opens his eyes, he sees that the sun is shining more brightly than ever. And he sees people everywhere.

At first he doesn't know where to look. His eyes wash over all the faces as if he is studying a painting, searching for its meaning. And then he sees them. Two people, a small halo of space surrounding them. And the light shining on the pair is that little bit brighter than elsewhere.

They are looking at something on the ground. A squirrel, Cliff realises, as he watches the two men watching the squirrel and he watches the squirrel watching the two men. And then the grey creature skips off. The two men turn to each other and laugh.

As they turn, Cliff can see their faces properly and they strike him as being terribly familiar. It doesn't take him long to place them as Jack and himself in their younger years. He does not entertain the possibility that they are anyone else. He sees them as Jack and himself.

I am sure. I am positive, Cliff thinks. *I have never been more certain of anything else in my entire life.*

He sees people *everywhere*. Young couples, old couples, single people, dog-walkers and a juggler.

Cliff shakes his head, sending tears running haphazardly across a fragile smile.

A juggler?!

Everyone is going about their own business and the two men walk off hand in hand. And not one person turns to look at them. No one stops, no one stares. No one turns.

And it is beautiful.

Is it Her?

by

Kath Middleton

Frank

1

IS IT HER?

It must be. I'd know that jaunty walk anywhere.

She always loved bright colours and I see she still has that scarlet coat. How very like her to team it with a bright umbrella. She wore red constantly back in that golden summer seven years ago. The summer before the war.

Was it really as golden as it seems in my memory? It's funny that past summers are always soaked in sunshine, though no doubt we had our share of thunderstorms and sudden floods. The nights back then were always black and their skies were star-sprinkled. Winters were bright and crisp. We create the past in our memories. Is Vera only in my past? In my memory?

So much happened in those seven years. I've come back to look for her but I know she's not the girl I left behind and I'm not the man she waved off. We parted in the sunshine. If that's her, we'll be meeting this time in a thunderstorm.

I really got to know her in 1939. Before that she'd only been Harry Conway's little sister. Harry was my best friend at school, brought together as we were by the fact that my surname is Bridges and we were consecutive in the register. Most of the time it was just the two of us, out on our bikes on a Sunday afternoon. By then, Vera had changed from being an annoying little sister to being a creature of beauty and fascination. She made me blush. She made me foolish and tongue-tied and initially I resented that.

Over that summer, we took our Sunday afternoon picnics seriously, Harry and I. I was currently working in my father's shop but, after taking night classes, I now had a place on a course in the autumn to study accountancy. I'd be the first in my family to have letters after my name. Harry, always good with his hands, was an engineering apprentice. We both worked long hours but we knew how to let it all go when the weekend came.

We'd grab some bread and cheese, maybe a bottle of beer each, and bike down to the dunes. It was so restful to watch the sea. After we'd eaten, we'd lie on the dune sand propped on one elbow, trying to avoid the prickly marram grass, and we'd chat and laugh and joke. I'm quite ashamed to remember how rarely we spoke about the politics of the day. The dark cloud that loomed over all our futures. We were simply looking the other way.

As the summer wore on, Vera began to join us

for some of these jaunts. She'd received a bicycle for her 17th birthday and was keen to get some mileage in. She didn't like beer, though. Her drink of choice was dandelion and burdock.

She was a keen observer of what was being reported in the papers. Far more knowledgeable than we were.

"Aren't you worried, though?" she asked us on one occasion as we were laughing at some trivial event in the local town.

"About what?" we asked, almost simultaneously.

"About the war. There's one coming, you know. Everyone says so. At least, everyone who thinks and reads." She did that thing of lowering her head and looking at us through her fringe.

This was the first time Harry appeared to have taken the idea seriously.

"I'm not surprised he hasn't taken this in," she said, nodding at her brother, "but I thought someone like you, Frank, someone intellectual, might have been worried."

I vacillated between annoyance with myself at not having taken notice of what the papers were saying and being flattered out of my mind that Vera thought me an intellectual. I had the insouciance of youth but eventually even I had to admit that it was possible a conflict was looming.

"What about Mr Chamberlain?" I asked. "Last year he came back from the Munich Agreement talking of 'peace for our time'. If we go to war now, it'll have been a jolly short time, won't it?"

We were disinclined to agree on the dangers, she taking it all seriously and Harry and I still preferring to shrug it off. We didn't discuss it much more. The lovely, long summer afternoons and evenings we shared made us want to be agreeable to one another. I think Harry noticed something growing between his sister and his friend before we did. He told me later that he and she would simply have argued to the point of sulking about the likelihood of a global conflict occurring but she was holding back because of me. She didn't want to upset me. I was charmed by the very idea.

Eventually, she and I began to meet in the evenings once or twice a week. The light still remained in the sky until late and I formed the habit of picking her up in my father's car to whisk her away for a walk on the downs. I'd learned to drive his car the previous year. Not many people had one but he felt it was useful for a shopkeeper to be able to deliver and he saw me as a useful delivery boy, though at twenty, I bridled at the thought of being any kind of boy.

I'd park somewhere high up, with a view over the farmland dropping towards the glittering sea. We would hold hands and walk through wildflower-studded grass, laughing at the sheep and listening to the birds, like the love-struck young people we were. It was on one of those warm, insect-buzzing walks that we decided we would marry, as soon as she was old enough.

Harry knew all about this. He was my confidant and best friend. It made it slightly awkward that he was also my paramour's older brother but we laughed our way through the awkwardness. We didn't tell anyone else but he said he would be our best man if we wanted that. By the time we'd decided we'd marry, the clouds had really begun to gather over the continent of Europe and war began to look inevitable.

"Will you wait for me if I have to fight?" I asked.

"Of course I will. Who else would I want?"

We were sitting in our own separate living rooms when we heard the announcement on the wireless.

"This morning the British Ambassador in Berlin handed the German Government a final note saying that, unless we heard from them by 11 o'clock that they were prepared at once to withdraw their troops from Poland, a state of war would exist between us. I have to tell you now that no such undertaking has been received and that consequently this country is at war with Germany."

That stopped the nation in its tracks. It's one thing to know something will inevitably happen, like the death of a very old family member, but when it does, it's still a bombshell. And this announcement brought bombshells more than we could possibly imagine.

2

THE NATION was in shock. There were plenty of doom-mongers and at the time we thought they were looking on the black side. We didn't know how right they were. Then there were those who tried to pooh-pooh the dread we felt. It would soon be sorted out, they said, and Herr Hitler would see sense. Hindsight is wonderful.

Eventually it became obvious even to the worst deniers that war was here to stay and nobody could remain unaffected. The wave of patriotism carried us all on its crest and some of us decided that we'd volunteer rather than wait to be called up. I think I was buoyed by Vera's fervour as much as my own desire for natural justice when I applied for the air force. Harry applied too; he knew that he wouldn't be called up because engineering was a reserved occupation.

We turned up with a host of other young hopefuls and were given a medical. Harry was failed on his eyesight.

"I'm only a bit short-sighted, mate. They'll never notice," he'd told me. But they did. For the first time, he and I were separated. "But we can write," he assured me. "We'll keep in touch, whatever happens."

Vera switched rapidly between telling me she was proud of us and turning pale with terror. She feared for my life, which admittedly, I did too. I had never flown before but I wanted to make the big gesture. The flying missions seemed so much grander than crouching on battlefields, firing rounds and, in effect, hiding half the time.

I was sent for a ten-week initial training course in Newquay, Cornwall. After this, we were sorted into our abilities and undertook further training in those specialities. I wasn't chosen for pilot training but would act as Wireless Operator doubling as Air Gunner, a combination of roles we called WOp/AG. I wouldn't fly in the sense that I wouldn't pilot the plane but I would be aircrew and on completion of my training I was promoted to Sergeant.

I was part of the crew of a Wellington and assigned to Bomber Command. They said that if you survived the first five missions you then had a 50/50 chance with subsequent sorties. The danger was ever-present and I think we survived mainly on patriotic excitement. Most crews had a second pilot. It was usually someone who was in training and covered another post too. They soon stopped sending two fully-trained pilots on missions because if the plane went down, two pilots were lost.

The Wellingtons were built on a geodesic framework which meant that a plane and its crew could limp home even if a substantial part of the fuselage had been blown away. Those who flew in them came to love them, even though the later Lancasters got the better press. I shall never forget the day, in training, when George, our bomb aimer, was about to leave the plane.

The pilot, an experienced man, pulled him back and told him never to leave a plane until both propellers had stopped rotating. "I saw a man in another crew dash off out of the plane while one prop was still turning. It caught him and smashed his head like a burst balloon. I've seen some sights in my life but that haunted my sleep for weeks, I can tell you."

That story was a better lesson than any amount of shouting and bawling at us.

They liked a crew to bond so we had one or two changes and shuffles before we settled to a group who worked well together. The pilot was Johnny Shaw. Even now, only six years later, I can't believe we were all so young. He was twenty, like me, and the lives of the whole crew were in his hands. George Dawson was the bomb aimer and second pilot. He was a Canadian and as good a lad as you could hope to serve with. I was Wireless Operator and Air Gunner. We had two other gunners, one of whom was navigator much of the time. There were five in our little group, though some Wellingtons were crewed with six.

Our first missions were to fly over Germany dropping leaflets. It was part of the propaganda war but it also gave inexperienced crews the chance to get used to one another and to build up their experience. We were all enthusiastic and, at that age, convinced we were invincible but I'll admit to counting those first five missions before I felt more comfortable.

Adrenaline and patriotic fervour fuelled us, but I still felt fear crawling in my stomach and was only light-hearted when I heard George shout, "Bombs gone," and I knew we were turning for home. We would fly back over the downs where Vera and I had so recently lain together in the turf and promised one another our futures. It was only months before but it was another world I looked back on.

We air crew were allowed a week's leave every six weeks. It was an acknowledgement of the dangers of our role. We were given a return rail pass, so I was able to see Vera and Harry regularly. I also think that behind this generosity, the war office was ensuring we lads remembered what and whom we were fighting for. The time home was blissful. My mother spoiled me and although rationing was introduced, mothers all seemed to hoard their coupons ready for sons and daughters coming home on leave.

Naturally, I spent as much of my time as I could with Vera. I was giddy with the knowledge that for a whole week I didn't live in the terror of death. Only when the constant dread was lifted did I realise how it had coloured my days. The last day of every leave brought a black cloud with it, far worse than the one which settled on a Sunday night when I was a schoolboy.

We talked of engagement but the war was so oppressive, so dangerous that it sank our plans before we had even floated them. We parted each time with a kiss and a promise. "I'll wait for you," she would say, with tears in her lovely eyes.

3

SOME OF OUR SQUADRON acted as though they were invincible. They didn't seem to believe they could die. Either that, or they were better actors than I was. Each time I went out with dread crawling like a snake in my belly, and only when George shouted that the bombs had been dropped did I dare to think I had life after this mission.

I know this makes me sound like a miserable beggar but I wasn't. The camaraderie was wonderful. Nothing brings a group of lads together so much as the prospect of sudden and probably nasty death. We may have flown in fear but we returned jubilant. We had fun. It was one long party punctuated by bombing raids over Germany. I wrote to Vera after every flight to tell her we'd landed safely. In those months, our letters were our life-line. The oxygen we breathed. They were what I lived for.

Sadly, we knew that each bombing raid we returned from brought us inevitably closer to the one we wouldn't. Crews were blown out of the air, and literally never knew what had hit them. Some of the planes were downed behind enemy lines. Some, a sad group, limped all the way home only to crash on our own soil. So close to home.

Our number was up as we were returning from an attack on Munster. The Wellington was damaged beyond our ability to fly it home and Johnny, our pilot, took the decision to bail. As we jumped one by one, I could see the lads before me and behind me deploying their chutes and coming down like dandelion clocks into the fading afternoon. Because of the speed of the plane, we each made landfall some distance apart and had agreed to try to make our way home individually.

I came down to earth and tried to steer my parachute between the trees I could see below me. I really would have preferred an open space but I had to do my best. I drifted down into a small copse on the side of a hill. My chute caught on the upper branches and I couldn't get myself down. I tried swinging from side to side but I couldn't drop to the ground still attached to the chute. Leaving it up there was a signal that an airman had come down and there'd be a hue and cry on. I was high in the canopy but unless I stayed up here for the duration I would have to unfasten the harness and risk the drop. I hit the clasp with my hand and fell.

I tried to curl and roll but the distance I fell wasn't enough to allow that. I heard a snap, like a broken twig, and a fierce pain ran up my leg. I'd broken my ankle. I was done for. A huge, flapping parachute signalled my position and I could do no more than hop away. I stood, feeling sick with pain and shock, but without something to support me – something to use as a crutch – I couldn't move at all on this hilly ground. Capture seemed inevitable. I sat by the tree and awaited my fate.

Shortly, I saw a small figure approaching. A boy, pulling a bogie – a home-made cart with four wheels and a crate fastened on to enable him to pull things behind him. A child's version of a wheelbarrow, perhaps. He was carefully tugging a load of firewood behind him, taking great care not to tip it out on the rutted ground. He looked up and forward, and spotted me, sprawled on the ground, almost at his feet. I don't know which of us was the more frightened.

He backed off a pace or two, then, jabbering in German, he carefully approached me with a stout stick held out before him. A lunge and a jab and he was able to confirm that I was no threat to him. I could barely defend myself from his stick and certainly couldn't offer him any violence in return. Not that I could countenance attacking a child, not even a child of the enemy.

"Frank," I said, tapping myself on the chest. "Frank."

"Franz?"

"Frank."

"Frank?"

I gave him the thumbs-up and he gifted me with a smile.

"Klaus!" he announced, similarly indicating himself.

"Guten abend, Klaus," I managed, stretching my vestigial German to its limits. Convinced by my pantomime act, Klaus once again ran off into a long monologue and I lost him totally. He looked a question at me and then appeared to realise that my linguistic skills were not up to following him.

"You haf," he began, then bent to smack himself on the ankle, "leg? Hurt leg?"

I nodded and struggled to stand on my good foot.

"My prisoner," he indicated, waving his hand at me. "I take… capture?"

"Captive," I confirmed, wondering what the hell I was doing assisting this boy in taking me prisoner.

Klaus removed the sticks from his cart, piling them safely behind the big tree. The tree still waving its warning flag that an airman had dropped straight into it. Like an expert, he shinned up into the branches and unhooked the lines which held it fast. He dropped the chute to the ground and carefully rolled it all up. The silk was valuable, of course. The spoils of war.

"Come." He waved to his bogie and indicated in the most imaginative pantomime that he would help me to sit in it. What the hell. I couldn't stay here and I couldn't walk away.

He put his shoulder under my armpit and I hobbled the couple of yards to my conveyance. Clumsily, I dropped onto the rolled parachute and hefted my damaged leg ahead of me, resting it on the edge of the crate. In this undignified manner, I jolted and winced my way down the hillside and towards the outer buildings of a smallholding on the edge of the village in the distance.

We reached an outhouse of some sort, which, when he opened the door, I could see was a woodshed, no doubt the intended destination of the load of wood he had evicted by the tree. My small captor indicated that I should go inside.

"Prisoner," he said again, grinning at me. He helped me to stand, then we walked and hopped into the dark little shed, which was half filled with chopped logs and big bundles of deadfall sticks.

He knew I couldn't run off, but even so, he shut and apparently locked the door behind him, saying, "I come again," as he left me standing on one leg, alone in the dark. I had nowhere to sit, no light to see by - in a woodshed there's no need for a window. After what seemed a long time but was doubtless only fifteen minutes or so, I heard the door open again and the boy stood, silhouetted against the sunset. He had a bundle in his arms.

He came in and shook it out on the floor. It was a sleeping bag, and none too clean at that. It appeared to be the survivor of many boyhood games but it would do. It would have to. He began to move the logs, to redistribute them in the shed, so that there was a space behind the pile where he finally placed the sleeping bag, out of immediate sight of the door. I lay down there, reasonably comfortably, and he once again left and returned later with a couple of rough blankets and a paper bag with food in. Bread and some kind of cheese, but nothing has ever tasted so good.

I pointed to my ankle, and said, "Splint," miming wrapping something around it to tie it to a stick, which I'd foraged out of the nearest bundle. Eventually he understood and came back with a length of bandage, so I was able to immobilise the break.

I spent the night in that shed, cold and in pain, but I dozed on and off as the night progressed. How long would he keep me here? He seemed gleeful about having a prisoner of war – a pet one of his own. He looked around nine or ten years of age. It must have been an adventure to him, but all I could think of was how long it would be before his parents discovered his latest game and I was turned over to the authorities.

4

KLAUS MANAGED to keep me hidden in the shed and, more cleverly in wartime, adequately fed, for several weeks. I got up to sit on the logs in the day – which I was only able to differentiate from night by the light or lack of it which followed him in on his regular visits. I think the food situation was eased for his family by the fact that they were evidently growing or raising foodstuffs here. It wasn't a farm, not being on a big enough scale but my senses told me they had pigs and chickens and I knew they grew vegetables.

I was brought food and water every morning before Klaus set off for school, and every evening after he had eaten, he returned with more. My other daily needs were catered for via a bucket which he removed and returned cleaned out each evening. It wasn't easy in the first few weeks.

We tried out our language skills on each other and managed to communicate reasonably well, though much of it was on the level of charades. I came to understand that he and his mother were running the place because his father was away fighting the British. Most of the time I was able to forget that he and I were on opposing sides in a deadly fight. We struck up a great friendship and I looked forward to his arrival each time, regardless of the food it ensured.

My ankle began to heal, though I think I'll always have a slight limp. I could eventually bear some weight on it and I made a point of exercising in the day, up and down the length of the shed once I could walk a little. I also tried lifting progressively heavier logs of wood and doing press-ups in my little space behind the wall of firewood. Klaus was very good at keeping the supplies topped up and filling the log basket in the house so his mother never had to come here looking for kindling. He made daily excursions into the wood for sticks and branches and I could sometimes hear him chopping logs.

His mother, 'Mutti' was called Gertrud and 'Vatti' was Walther, surname Drechsler. From what I could gather, Walther was a great supporter of Hitler and his ideology. Klaus supported Germany but in the way rival gangs of boys have their own gang's interest at heart. He wasn't yet old enough to be sucked into the politics behind the conflict.

I sometimes thought I'd be here until the war ended. The days, tedious though they were, followed on from one another. I could only detect the change of season by the fact that it became almost too cold to sleep at night. Klaus promised me another blanket if he could sneak one away.

Then came the day I knew would happen. The day I dreaded and feared. I heard his mother humming in the yard. It went on for some time and when it finally stopped I thought she'd gone away. But then I heard her footsteps approaching my hideout.

As she unfastened the door, I shrank back behind the wall of logs, only realising as I did so that the end of my sleeping bag still stuck out into the little

gap we'd left for access. I usually rolled it up to give
me walking and exercise space in the daytime but
today I'd just kicked it out of the way. I'd become
slack.

Frau Drechsler began to fill a basket with logs
and some of the smaller kindling that Klaus had
brought in from the woods. I didn't dare to breathe as
I heard her dropping logs into her basket. I couldn't
see her without showing myself and I hoped she'd
miss the tell-tale corner of the sleeping bag, or think it
was some game of Klaus's and ignore it.

She did neither. I heard her tutting, then she
came around the side of the wall Klaus had carefully
built and I had continued to maintain. Our eyes met.
She shrieked and dropped her basket. What a sight I
must have looked. Klaus occasionally brought me a
basin and washcloth but I'd not shaved in months. I
must have looked like the wild man of the woods. A
wild man wearing a shabby, no doubt smelly but
unmistakably British airman's uniform.

Klaus must have been out in the yard seeing to
the pigs or the hens. At any rate, he was here pretty

quickly and his face betrayed his horror at his mother's finding out who was sharing their woodshed. There followed a rapid exchange in over-excited German which I was completely unable to follow. I sat on my log chair. There was no point in my doing anything else. I could now use my broken ankle but it wasn't yet strong enough for me to run, even for a short sprint, or to attempt the sort of long walk I'd need to reach friendly territory. My immediate future was in her hands.

After a great deal of talking, some gesticulating and, to my surprise, the occasional laugh, Frau Drechsler and Klaus beckoned me out of the dark room in which I'd existed for nearly two months. They led me, dazzled by the light, to the back door of the house where we entered a plain but scrubbed kitchen, sweetly warm and redolent of new bread. I didn't know how long I'd be here but I had been let out of hell and given a glimpse – and the scent – of heaven.

Still talking in rapid German, the Frau led me to a door in the kitchen wall, and down some steps into a cellar. Either this was my temporary holding cell until the authorities came for me, or I was exchanging the frigid, wood-scented shed for a warmer prison. I stood, listening to them jabbering, while Klaus and his mutti brought a folding camp-bed and warmer bedding than I'd previously enjoyed. She brought me a hot drink and bade me sit on the folding bed while she attempted to talk to me and ask me some questions.

She had only school-girl English but it was better than her son's English or my German and we got along a little better. She told me her name, I told her mine, although Klaus had already imparted this information to us. From his demeanour, he was excited to be sharing his 'pet' prisoner with his mother. I had been expecting the marching boots of an escort party to whisk me away but she seemed to accept my presence and to tolerate it, at the very least.

"Frank, you are the prisoner of Klaus?" she asked.

"Ja." I tried to speak in their language when I could. It seemed only polite.

"You stay here. Be my prisoner!" she announced with a smile, as though it were the obvious solution. I began to ask in fragmented German, then gave up and switched to what I hoped was simplified English, why she was taking this risk. If her son had been caught giving help and hospitality to an enemy, it would be dismissed as a child's prank or game, much though it may be frowned upon and even punished. If an adult did it, she would be subjected to severe punishment, even incarceration in a camp, from the rumours I'd heard. What would happen to Klaus then?

Slowly, and with difficulty on both our parts, she explained that her grandmother was Jewish. That automatically made her mother and her Jewish too, as it followed the female line. Jewish people were being captured and imprisoned in their own country, the place they'd lived in for generations in some cases. I hadn't realised that things had got so bad. I tried to ask about Herr Drechsler but she shrugged. He would be angry with her. From the look on her face, he would be more than angry. I offered to give myself up but she wouldn't hear of it.

From then onwards, although I was kept in the cellar, behind a lot of big, spider-haunted packing cases, I was warm and was much better fed. Before, Klaus had been bringing me bread and left-overs. Now I received a good meal with the fresh vegetables from their smallholding. There was a skylight, too, and although it was made of the sort of thick, greenish glass that you could walk on, it allowed some light into my life. I still missed seeing the sky. My days on the downs with Vera seemed so far off, days during which we'd had long views of the rolling slopes of down-land, the distant sea and the massive sky above us.

I was sure that Vera and Harry would now have been told that I was missing in action. If some of the crew had made it back home, it may well be assumed that I was dead. I couldn't contact anyone at home and had no means of informing my family and friends that I was still alive – for the moment.

All this ended when Herr Drechsler came home on leave.

5

THE FIRST I KNEW was a hurried tramping of feet on the cellar steps and Klaus came dashing into my little sanctuary like a tidal wave. I had to slow him down before I could even make out a word.

"Mein Vater. Vatti. My father is home! We... move your bed and... put in big box. Put you in box too?"

"You want me to hide?" Bloody silly question. The boy was frantic.

"Ja. Hide, yes. Vatti will find you if he comes here. He does not usually come. But if he does. If he finds you..." He waved his hand between the two of us.

"We are both in trouble?" I asked.

He nodded, bit his lip and dashed a tear away from his eye.

"And your mother?" Another nod.

"I'll hide everything. You go. I'll say I broke in and you didn't know I was here."

I watched as he processed my words and then he nodded again and left me in the cellar, my heart thudding with fear, not only for myself but for the kind pair who had looked after me – an enemy of their country. I expected to be rumbled within moments but of course, the soldier returning on leave for a few days wasn't going to inspect his home in minute detail for the possible presence of enemy personnel. Why would he? I hurriedly hid all traces of my habitation here and I tipped a big packing crate on its side so I could crawl inside and pull the lid behind me if I heard someone on the steps.

My big problems were food and water and the ever-present bucket. I kept it covered with a blanket but now placed it inside a packing case and closed the lid. If it had to stay there for five days I felt sure its vile odour would betray me. With his father home, even for a few days, Klaus couldn't come to me with fresh bread or a drink at regular intervals, as he had been doing, and certainly couldn't take away the bucket. Gertrud had even slipped me little treats when she'd been baking. I understood her apparent friendliness to be little more than a horror of what was happening in her native land to people like her, people of Jewish extraction. She must feel safe here with her husband, I thought, but she wouldn't want to rock the boat by having me discovered in her cellar.

It must have been late on the second day that I heard feet coming down the cellar steps. I hid in my packing crate. To be honest, I'd barely stepped a couple of paces away from it since Klaus had told me his father was home.

"Frank?" came a hoarse whisper. It was my young friend with a thick sandwich and a bottle of water for me. I thanked him heartily. I was afraid the loud grumbling of my insides would have given me away if his father had come down here patrolling. He told me he would come when he could but it wouldn't be so often.

"How long will your father be home?" I asked. It took him a while to get his head around the tenses but he finally told me that Herr Drechsler had a five-day pass. Three more days. As long as he didn't decide to inspect his cellar, I could perhaps get away with it.

I would have given anything for some books to read but all Klaus could offer were in German. My knowledge of the language was not sufficient to allow me to get any use from them. I sat, hunched, bored and hungry, for two more days until once again, Klaus pattered down into my dim hidey-hole and presented me with a sandwich and water. I longed to sink my teeth into the dark thick bread but my stomach clenched for want of water so I took a long pull at the bottle first of all.

"Vatti... he look for me," said Klaus, retrieving the previous bottle and rushing back outside. I hoped he wasn't going to get into trouble for this. No sooner had I formed the thought than I heard a deep voice booming from the top of the stairs.

"Klaus?" was the first word. I lost track after that as the boy and his father engaged in a rapid-fire conversation, Klaus quickly retreating back up the concrete steps as his father clattered his way down. I crept back into my crate before he could focus on my dim corner.

I couldn't understand what was said but it became obvious to me that Herr Drechsler had followed his son as he'd crept through the cellar door carrying food and water. He could now plainly see that the boy had only an empty bottle with him and couldn't possibly have eaten the food himself in that short time. The game was up.

With just one day of his leave remaining, Walther Drechsler stormed down the steps of his cellar and began kicking open the packing crates. He found my camp bed and the old but serviceable blankets his wife and son had given me. Their very presence in the cellar implicated Drechsler's family in hiding and aiding me. At that point, I knew there was nothing to be gained from continuing to crouch in my box. I stood, lifting my hands high above my head, and gave myself up as his prisoner.

I emerged around the corner the pile of crates and stared into the barrel of a gun. It seemed the soldier in Walther Drechsler was never off duty. He sent Klaus into the farmhouse to procure a length of rope with which he tied my hands securely behind my back and lashed my ankles together too. I was going nowhere now. I couldn't eat my sandwich either. My mouth watered and my stomach rumbled with longing for it.

But I would have bigger things to worry about now than food or water. Herr Drechsler summoned the local Gestapo and, my legs untied, I was marched away. I could guess where I would be going. They could see I was an airman from the ragged remains of my uniform and I was certain I was bound for one of their Prisoner of War camps, of which I had heard nothing good.

To my great sorrow, the man – the apology for a man – also turned his wife and young child over to the Gestapo for harbouring an enemy. I was prodded and herded onto a flatbed truck and taken away, but not before I saw the doleful sight of Klaus and Gertrud being shoved into another truck, tied at the wrists, to be taken who knew where.

6

THE WAR was over for me at that point. I spent the rest of it incarcerated in a camp but, from the little rumour which reached our ears, I had no hope that any better treatment awaited my young friend Klaus and his mother. They had shown me kindness and I came to realise that they, too, would be interned for the duration of the war.

I am unable to understand a man who holds his political beliefs to be more dear to him than the welfare, even the life, of his wife and young son. I have shed bitter tears for that small boy and his gentle mother, far more so than for my fellow prisoners. We were treated harshly but were at least fed and kept alive. The camps where enemy forces were interned were subject to inspection under the Geneva Convention so we didn't fare too badly. It was dismal, often cold and we were invariably hungry but it was something to get through, and we did.

Sadly, the camps which held those nationals accused of aiding the enemy were not so inspected.

I will not dwell on my time in that camp. Several of us made escape attempts but few of these had any success and generally the men who tried were marched back in and subjected to worse treatment, though we all cheered them on their return.

I am skating over this period of my war – I know others have done so too. It isn't a thing on which we choose to dwell. I dare say many a man will go to his grave without sharing, even with his dearest friends and closest relatives, the atrocities of war to which they were subjected. The daily, dismal grind which continued without hope and without apparent end. Sufficient to say that it changed us utterly. We are not the young, carefree boys who joined up when war was declared.

Eventually, the war was won and we were liberated. I made enquiries about the Drechsler family but I couldn't find out anything about them. I eventually discovered where they'd been taken but by the time the allied forces had reached the place, there were very few alive there. My fears for their safety were well founded.

I never thought I could harbour personal hatred for a man but I do for Walther Drechsler. I don't even know if he survived the war. I hope not, yet if he did, I hope what he did, in the service of a man and an ideal which proved to be so evil, returns daily to haunt him and destroy his peace.

Naturally, since I was reported missing, presumed dead, I received no further mail from home. I had failed to get messages back to the family, too. I fell through the Red Cross net and subsequently discovered that I was not the only prisoner mourned by his family while he spent the war in an internment camp. My own family believed I had perished, as too did Harry and Vera. They had both been faithful correspondents. On my return to Britain I wrote to Vera and to Harry but never received any reply. My father informed me that their house had been bombed but he believed they had all survived, in an Anderson shelter in the back garden.

I went to see the house but could scarcely recognise it. Streets I had known and grown up in had missing houses, just like a youngster might have a tooth missing from an otherwise gleaming row. The spaces, called crofts by the children I found playing there, were beginning to be colonised by clumps of nettles and stands of rose-bay willow-herb.

My mother took me gently to one side and sat me down. She told me that, understanding me to be dead, Vera had married. My mother had lost touch with the family after they moved from the bombed-out house. I was initially angry. How could my beloved, the girl I was hoping to marry, do such a thing? The one thought which had kept me going in times of despair was Vera's promise to wait for me till the war was over.

Then, stopping to think a little more clearly, I realised that Vera, along with my own family, must have received that news which all families and loved ones of serving soldiers, sailors and airmen fear the most. She, like my own parents, was told I was missing in action. I found out that three of my fellow crew had managed to get home safely. My family were later sent a telegram to inform them that I was presumed dead. She had grieved, no doubt, as did my parents and younger sister. But, war is war and we live for the day. I began to see that, being comforted by one of Harry's workmates, another engineer in a reserved occupation, she would eventually let go of my memory and find love. I could not have asked the poor girl to mourn me forever. I was determined to find her, though. I wanted to give her a farewell kiss.

Ex-servicemen and women could search for missing friends. There were organisations to help them do that. Nobody was helping us to find those who'd gone missing on the home front, though. I contacted as many of my old friends as I could find when I got home. Some, naturally, had fallen in the war. Some had passed their war in Britain in various activities and, like the Conway family, had lost their homes due to enemy action.

I discovered from another old classmate that Harry had been injured in the air-raid and was still recovering in a hospital for those with severe spinal injuries. It was hoped that he would eventually walk again but the road ahead for him was still a long one and he couldn't yet receive visitors other than his immediate family. I wrote to him but the reply came back written by a nurse. She told me that Harry was overjoyed to hear that I was alive but as he remained flat on his back and would be so for some time, he was unable to write back. He evidently dictated some notes to her as they were written as a reporter would write – he says... he thinks... The final remarks were that he looked forward immensely to being able to receive visitors and seeing me in person and that I should look for Vera in Ayling, a small village not far from my own home. Sadly, his dictated note didn't offer an address, but I knew Ayling with its cluster of houses and its small village square. I ought to have been able to find her there.

So, here I am, in my father's car and my itchy demob suit. It's a cold day and I've got an overcoat on too. I probably look sinister but I'm sure she'll recognise me. And as I pull round the corner, there's the lithe figure in the bright coat. Without seeing the face I'd know it was Vera. I would have said 'my Vera' but I haven't that right now. She's someone else's wife.

We were innocent children as we lay on the downs, the summer before the war, kissing and holding hands and promising our futures to one another. We lay, little understanding what our world was becoming, amongst the down-land sheep which echoed the fleecy sky. Who ever knows what's coming? I'm not the Frank she knew. My wartime experiences have seen to that. And she will not be the Vera I fell in love with. She's a married woman now. Some lucky fellow, another friend of her brother Harry's, has the right to call her his wife. She may even have a child.

I tentatively wave to the girl in the distance. She has seen me and waves back. Does she know who it is?

Do I?

It's Vera, yes, but is it *still* her?

Vera

1

THAT LOOKS JUST LIKE... but can it be? His parents showed me the telegram which said he was presumed dead. Oh... but is it him? I've stopped to look as he's got out of the car – and that little dog's watching him too! What an awful wet and miserable day to meet the person who's haunted your dreams for seven long years. If it's him. But... he died. I saw the telegram. I've never trusted a knock at the door since that day.

It seems so long ago now, but it's only seven years since Harry's best friend Frank Bridges began courting me. He and Harry used to go out on their bicycles and would often disappear for a whole afternoon. At seventeen, I was inquisitive enough to wonder what on earth they got up to and determined enough that I eventually found out. Actually, it wasn't as exciting as I'd thought – cycling along the lanes, lying in the grass, talking and occasionally picnicking on bread and cheese.

I did the little sister thing of making myself such a nuisance that my mother eventually said, "Why don't you take her along with you, Harry? A good cycle ride will tire her out." I wasn't best pleased to think that the only reason my mother could provide was that it would tire me. I presume this meant I'd spend the rest of the evening out of my brother's hair rather than in it.

"She'll have to keep up," he said. "We can't be hanging around waiting for my kid sister."

"I can cycle as well as you," I said. I could be such a petulant brat when I wanted to be but I decided it wasn't in my interest to get his back up. "I can bake us a few buns if you like?" You could always get to Harry's heart through his stomach.

Eventually I was allowed to accompany them. Sunday afternoons could be stultifyingly tedious with my parents listening to the radio and little else to do.

They were a bit old-fashioned in their view of what was a suitable occupation on the Sabbath but fresh air and exercise were approved activities. I began making a snack for the three of us and tagging along with them.

They were typical young men of the time. They didn't take much notice of current affairs and when I began to ask them, in order to seem like the educated young woman not the ignorant little sister, their views on what was happening in Europe and what they thought the country's response should be, they looked at me as if I were speaking Martian.

"But everyone says there's a war coming," I said as they each gave me such a blank look I could have laughed. I might have if it hadn't been so serious.

For a while there, I thought I might have put Frank off by appearing to be such a blue-stocking as my father would call it. He rarely spoke directly to me on those first few Sunday rides. He'd known me forever, it seemed, as he'd progressed through school with my brother, a couple of years ahead of me. At senior school age, of course, we'd been segregated but he still came around to our house often enough for me to notice how he became less of the gawky, acne-splashed boy with the voice which cracked and changed as it broke, and more of the good-looking and muscular young man. I always thought he looked nice. He didn't have film-star looks but he was well-proportioned and had a smile I'd do anything for.

We were shy of each other to begin with. I would make my pseudo-intellectual comments about current affairs and Harry would pull my leg, whereas Frank would just smile. I never knew if he thought I was trying to be clever (which I was) or if he was smiling in encouragement. He smiled, though; that was all that mattered.

Eventually we became more comfortable with one another and, I don't know quite how, we became a couple. The three of us still did the Sunday afternoon picnic but as the summer wore on and the days lengthened, Frank would occasionally call around after work and take me to the downs, not to picnic, but to lean our bikes against a fence and walk through the close-cropped chalk-land grasses to watch the sheep and listen to the birds. Sometimes he'd call for me in the car he'd borrowed from his father and I felt so important, leaving the house to be whisked away in the sort of vehicle most people near us couldn't dream of owning. Thinking of what followed, those memories are golden.

I don't remember anything as formal as a proposal but we came to an understanding that, if war didn't come, if all that posturing from the politicians turned out to be hot air, then we would ask my parents' permission for us to be married. If war came, as seemed inevitable as that sunny summer grew older and its days shorter, then the boys both said they would join up. Frank leant towards the air force and, since Harry was in a reserved occupation, he wanted to volunteer for the same as Frank as he knew he wouldn't be called up to the army.

I know now that many young women of my age rushed headlong into marriage because they felt that they wanted to make a commitment which would be an anchor for them and their men in turbulent times. We didn't know how turbulent they would be, or how long they would last. Some, I now know, faced a horrific time of separation and they got back a husband they scarcely recognised; sometimes with physical injuries which changed their lives beyond anything they could have envisaged when they made their vows in those hurried marriages. Some of the men seemed whole on their return but bore invisible scars – shell shock or nightmares.

Girls like me married boys and either lost them, or saw them return as men. Haunted, broken men in some cases.

At the time, as we wandered hand in hand over the grass of summer evenings, picking a few wildflowers and gazing over the lustrous sea towards France, we shared the concern of the nation but it was tempered with the optimism of youth. It would all turn out fine, wouldn't it? The boys made jokes of it all, not really believing that they would soon be fighting a war.

Inevitably, we all heard the radio announcement which changed our lives. For many of those listening, it signalled the end of them.

2

THE COUNTRY was abuzz, like a poked beehive. Everyone thought and talked of nothing but the fact that we were at war with Germany. I had felt my heart thud when I'd heard the announcement, so baldly stated on the radio in my own living room. Unlike the boys, I'd seen it coming; I'd felt it to be inevitable. Though they'd shrugged it off, I felt a rush of fear to hear it said aloud.

We kissed and held hands as Frank announced that he would attend an air force interview. We promised we'd marry after the war – that our love would last forever and that I'd wait for his return, however long that would take. And when I said it, how fervently I meant it!

Frank and Harry set off determined that they would join the air force together. Comradeship was important in wartime and in the last war, the government had acknowledged this by recruiting 'Pals' regiments' to keep the young men together. Whole streets or factories would lose their lads of fighting age to join up into a group who would be prepared to fight all the harder to protect their friends. The downside of that was the desperate sadness when a street fell into deep mourning as they all lost sons and brothers, sweethearts and husbands in the same battle.

Still, we had learned our lessons from that conflict and I felt sure that the boys, if successful, at least wouldn't fly in the same plane. I began to realise there was a real possibility of losing one or both of these two young men who meant the world to me. At least I needn't have worried about them both coming down in one insane accident. Harry's slight short-sightedness showed up in the tests. None of the family realised he was short-sighted. I think he'd got quite clever at hiding the fact but he wasn't up to the air force standard so my lovely Frank joined up on his own.

I came home from work the day after he left and spent an age trying out my name on a doodling pad as Vera Bridges, Mrs V Bridges and other variants. I was so proud of him but I so wanted him back. I wanted our future together and, like a petulant child, I wanted it now.

I began to look forward to the post as I'd never done previously. If I heard the clack of the letterbox I'd rush down and sort out any letter for me and whisk it away to my bedroom to read it in secret. Of course, most of the time I wasn't at home when the post came so I found my letters from Frank on the mantelpiece which meant that my parents and Harry knew exactly how often Frank wrote. I wrote to him daily, the minutiae of my life here in a small town he knew already like his own face in the mirror. When he could, he wrote back just as often but of course, he began on his training and it wasn't always possible.

We said we'd tell each other everything but I'm sure he kept things back from me. It would be like him to underplay the dangers of his role. I think the trainers must have told them that it was important to keep their own and civilians' morale high. So, from the viewpoint of his letters, it was all laughing, tricks and practical jokes in preparation for their part in the war and I'm sure that wasn't the case. Naturally, you laugh and joke in dangerous times – it's whistling in the dark, isn't it? But they must have worked very hard and taken it all much more seriously than he made it sound.

Eventually, he finished the initial training course and sounded rather upset not to have been chosen for pilot training. He would continue training as a wireless operator, doubling up as air gunner when appropriate. It still sounded to me like a very important and responsible role. He kept telling me in his letters how vital every cog was in the machine. I'm not sure if he was trying to tell me or himself that WOp/AG, as he called it, was as important as pilot, but as far as I was concerned, they were all heroes.

When they eventually began flying real missions I lived in an unsustainable state of heart-in-mouth in the first week or so. As soon as they came back, Frank would write to me. I loved to get those letters. His first missions were to drop leaflets over the continent. Propaganda was important in wartime. As early as the middle of September 1939, the so-called Lord Haw Haw and his programme, Germany Calling, was aimed at the demoralisation of the British. Frank and his fellow crew members were on these easy missions initially. Of course, it didn't stop the enemy trying to shoot them out of the air. But they had no gun or bomb handling to do.

Because their work was acknowledged to be hard and dangerous, they were given a pass every six weeks or so and I counted the days till I saw him again. He sometimes came here even before he went to see his parents but of course, it depended on the time of day his train got in. We'd spend as long as we could together, just walking, holding hands and dreaming of the time we could do more.

"We'll be together soon," he'd say. "Jerry can't withstand our boys for too long. We'll win and then you and I can be together till we're old and wrinkly!" He could always make me laugh.

As time wore on, I heard the rumours that

Bomber Command had only a 50/50 chance of living till the end of their tour of duty. After successfully flying their full quota of missions they were given jobs in training more new airmen. The more I thought of this statistic the more anxious I became. I didn't want to write morbid letters so I tried to keep it all light when I told him what was going on here. I'd make fun of Harry who had to keep at it in his civilian job but would tell me stories of picking up girls in the cinema in the blackout and being horrified on getting outside to find that some of them were as old as our mother. Anything to keep cheerful. That was our way.

I began working in a munitions factory. I hated the thought that what I was doing was bringing death to people just like me in Germany. They couldn't all be as evil as Hitler, could they? But we had to do it. We had to keep our boys supplied with the bombs and ammunition they needed. We couldn't leave them vulnerable. Harry, unable to fight because of the nature of his work, tried to do his bit in a different way. He became an Air Raid Warden and took great pains to point out that there was so much more to this than shouting 'Put that light out' at regular intervals. I think those like him, supporting the war effort at home because of the importance of their jobs, had to make their civilian role sound important for their own self-esteem.

I made all these anecdotes from my own life and Harry's into funny stories to tell Frank. He wrote back with all the latest excitement, as much as he was able to tell. So much of their operations was secret but he could always concoct a story to make me laugh and to take some of the sting from our separation.

Then the letters stopped coming.

3

I DIDN'T get a letter every day, just after they'd returned from a raid, so initially I didn't notice. After a couple of days, I began to feel fearful. Harry kept telling me not to worry. "They might be on training again, you know. They don't tell everyone what they're doing. State secrets and all that. No point giving Jerry info. If mail's intercepted then the news gets into the enemy's hands – knowledge is power as they say. Don't worry, he'll just be somewhere brushing up on his semaphore or something."

Harry was unfailingly optimistic about this but when I visited the Bridges family to see if anyone there had heard from Frank, there was an exchange of glances which told me so much.

"No, Vera. We've not had a note from him since last Friday," his mum said. That was longer ago than I'd heard. "But this morning we had a telegram from the War Office to say that his Wellington had been shot down over Germany." I must have fainted at this point because I have no further memory of events until his mother was wafting me with a tea-towel as I sat by their kitchen table. "Here," she said, pressing a cup of tea into my hands. "Sip this. It'll help. They tell us that the crew parachuted out so we are still hopeful he could make his way home."

I felt so awful. His parents were comforting me and I felt that I should have been the one trying to cheer them. I think the tension, the waiting for each letter assuring me that the last bombing raid was a success and they were all home unharmed, had finally broken me down. I sat in their kitchen and sobbed.

"We'll let you know straight away if we hear anything else," Mr Bridges said. I nodded and pulled my coat tighter around my shoulders. I felt suddenly cold. I had lost my future and I didn't know what to do.

I carried on at work and at home but I knew I'd lost my sparkle. Everyone said so. A week passed, then two. I would pop around after work to see Mrs Bridges – the real Mrs Bridges, though I'd fantasised about signing my own name thus – to see if they'd had further news. We would have a cup of tea together but couldn't cheer one another up.

One day I arrived in the rain, feeling as low as I ever had since he went missing, and was surprised by a huge smile on Frank's mother's face. "Oh, Vera!" she said and I was sure she would tell me he was safe. "Their pilot, Johnny Shaw – he's managed to get back to England. He made it to the French border and the resistance got him out. He said they'd all parachuted out and they would all either get back, like he did, or be taken as prisoners of war."

"Oh, how awful. To be taken prisoner, I mean. Will we find out?"

"I think so. There are all these laws about how they have to treat enemy forces – the Geneva Convention, I believe – and of course the War Office will tell us if he gets back, like Johnny did. He'll be allowed a period of leave then."

I had to have hope. It was all I had. Over the

next few months news came in that the other lads had mostly made it back home. George Dawson had been captured as soon as he'd hit the ground and was now in a camp. His family had been informed and were able to get letters and even little food parcels to him. I'd hoped that had happened to Frank but as time lengthened it didn't seem that it had. He had just fallen off the face of the planet.

With dread, I faced the prospect that he'd been shot as his parachute descended. Or maybe his chute had failed and he'd hit the ground of a foreign country hard enough to break his body fatally. I was in despair. I gave myself up to my duties at work and joined Harry occasionally on his evening ARP watch. Anything to distract myself from the awful ache in my heart.

Then came the dreaded news. An official telegram to his parents stated that Francis Anthony Bridges was missing in action and presumed dead.

I went into mourning then. I wore my darkest clothes which was a feat in itself. I usually chose bright colours, yellow and red being favourites, but I had a dark suit which I sometimes wore for work and this became my standard outfit. Friends were kind and understanding but after a few weeks they began to urge me to snap out of it, to look to the future, telling me that was what Frank would have wanted. I knew exactly what he wanted and it was the same as I did. A future together – but that had been snatched away.

I realised that I wasn't alone in this. I was sharing in what a huge number of girlfriends, wives and mothers were going through. The nation was saturated in grief, once you scraped away the cheerful, patriotic surface. People dreaded a knock on the door – telegrams were delivered separately from the normal post. I knew I couldn't go on eating my heart out but it seemed disloyal to my first, and, I'd thought, only love, to think about living a life without him. But I had to.

Months dragged by and rationing began to kick in. We had to get used to the coupon system and people would exchange coupons or save them up for special occasions. My friend Margaret had a sweet tooth and I could give her my sugar ration in exchange for something else. We would occasionally have extra cheese or butter because of this.

Things carried on in the same way, day after day, month after month, so that it seemed we had always lived under this cloud. It was hard remembering that golden summer of '39 when this was all a dream – a nightmare. Now we lived with the threat of air-raids, with shortages of food, though people said that our diet was healthier. Perhaps so, but it felt like we might die of tedium.

4

EVENTUALLY, in an effort to drag me out of the doldrums, Harry invited me to join him at the pictures with two of his friends from work. He didn't mention at the time that Elsie was his current squeeze and Stan was a single man on the lookout. Stan, too, was exempt from call-up because his skills were needed at home for the war effort. When I turned up with my brother and met the two of them outside the Regal Cinema I assumed they were a couple. Then Harry leaned in to Elsie and gave her a very unbrotherly kiss and put a proprietorial arm around her shoulder.

"And this is Stan," he said, waving his free hand between us. "Stan, my sister Vera."

Harry sat between me and Elsie and Stan sat on my other side. We talked a little before the film began and he seemed friendly and polite. Then the whole place hushed as the Pathé News came with film clips of 'our brave boys' and I could barely hold it together. He gave the back of my hand such a gentle touch, barely brushing it, but it showed an understanding and sympathy which I soaked up like a desert soaks up moisture.

After that, he asked if he could see me again. He brought a little light to the dark places in my heart and I was glad of it. As we got to know one another over the following months I told him about Frank and what had become of him. He was understanding and I appreciated his strength. I never once felt he was taking advantage of my vulnerability. I began to realise that it's possible to love twice. He would never replace my Frank, but he was another good man and I loved him.

Before a year had passed, he asked me to marry him and my parents and Harry were overjoyed to see me happy again. My mother had her friends saving coupons so she could make a fruit cake for our wedding.

"Just because you're a war bride you're not

going to do without," she told me. "You've had a hard time, what with… everything… and you'll have the best we can manage."

Clothing coupons provided me with a white wedding dress to be proud of and Harry's Elsie was my bridesmaid. It wasn't the wedding I'd envisaged but it was a hopeful start on a new life. I worked hard to ensure that Stan didn't feel he was second best. Yes, he was my second choice but I loved him dearly and told him so often.

Housing was impossible to get as homes were bombed and people doubled up with family. Stan came to live with us and my parents moved furniture around to give us the biggest bedroom and allowed us the front parlour as our own sitting room. That made so much difference. We almost had a little flat of our own.

The skies were dark over Britain but my own sky was blue again. After six months of marriage, I found myself pregnant. Stan and I were expecting a child. My mother and father were beside themselves with joy and Uncle Harry revelled in his new role. At work, I felt I was nursing a secret to myself. I wasn't far on enough to show and I wanted to keep this news tightly curled up inside me for a few more weeks. Stan's mother and my own started knitting. Everything was in a neutral colour, of course. Lots of white, lemon and pale mint green. It was considered unlucky to try to predict but in my own mind, if this baby should be a boy, it would be called Francis. No doubt about it. And I knew that Stan wouldn't mind. He was a generous person and understood my longing for a connection with my old life – my pre-war life.

I began to believe we would get through this war. We'd been like this for years and I didn't know how we'd cope with the freedom, the luxury foods and the lack of that overarching fear we all lived with but I looked forward to finding out. Rumours were that we were winning the war in Europe and that it was only a matter of time.

Then, coming home from work one Thursday evening, looking forward to my mother's cooking and to greeting Stan before he went out on his night shift, I turned the corner into our road and stopped. The house wasn't there. Just the tumbled wall of the next door property showing charred wallpaper and rooms open to the evening air.

I stared in disbelief at the smoking ruins, the heaped bricks and burning wood, the funereal pall of smoke, which marked my home and the place my loved ones were gathered for an evening meal we would now not eat.

My memories of the next few hours are scrambled. I know I screamed. I screamed so hard I almost lost my voice for a day or two afterwards.

I rushed to the ruins of my childhood home. Had they all made it to the shelter in time? We'd heard the warning siren at work and had all rushed down into the cellar but the all-clear allowed us back up to continue our shift. Here, I could see no figures emerging from the back garden. Our neighbour came out of his partially demolished house with a look of deepest sorrow.

"What happened to them?" I asked. "Has anybody got out? Where are they?" I pushed past him and began to tear at the still-hot bricks with my bare hands. I wouldn't be dissuaded. I needed to feel I was doing something.

"They've taken them to hospital, Vera," he said. "Those who made it out."

5

I WOKE in a white room, with people in white garments peering over me as I lay on my back. I thought I'd died and I was in heaven and these drifting figures in snowy gowns were angels. One of them began to speak but I could make no sense of the words, which kept wowing in and out of hearing. Eventually, my surroundings resolved themselves into a hospital ward. I was in one of several beds, all containing people in various states of injury, most sporting bandages about some part of their person. I was out of place here.

"Lie still now," said a young girl with an Irish accent. Her lapel badge named her Breda. "You'll still be feeling a bit giddy if you try to get up just yet. You'll be up and about in no time."

Up and about? Then I remembered with a

slam the smoking ruins of my home.

"What happened in the air-raid? Why am I here? How are my family?"

"Shush now," she said gently. "That's a lot of questions. First things first. You were brought in this evening. You'd passed out trying to move bricks and such like on the bomb-site."

"It's not a bomb-site – it's my home," I cried, breaking down as memory returned.

"Sure it isn't anyone's home now, darling. But you had started to bleed. I'm sorry to have to tell you, but you've lost the baby too." Too? Who else had I lost? "Please," I said, almost too numb to cry for my lost child's future. "Who else? What happened?"

She sat by my bed and picked up my hand in hers. "Your parents made it to the shelter," she said. "Two young men seemed to be hanging around in the house. Your mother thinks they were trying to save belongings." At this, her eyes left mine and dropped to the crisp sheet which covered me. She looked up at me again, swallowing before she spoke. "One of them had a bag of baby-clothes in his arms. He was trapped under a fallen wall." She kept patting my hand, as though that would help. "He's alive, but he's very badly injured. He's been rushed to another hospital with a spinal surgery specialist. They'll do the very best for him. Try not to worry yourself, now."

"And the other young man? Did he get out? Please, tell me, Breda!"

Again, she dropped her eyes. "I'm sorry, love," she said, tears glittering on her lower lids. "One died in the rubble. They got him out but... it was too late. I'm so sorry."

I tried to discover which of the lads had got out and which had died. From the sound of the baby clothes, Stan was in hospital and Harry, my best friend and mentor all my life, must have been killed. I broke down again. I'd lost my baby and my brother and I became, for a moment, hysterical. Breda did the best thing she could have done. She hugged me, stroked my hair and gave me a sedative. I slept. Badly – but I slept.

Next day my parents came in to visit me and I was told I could go home that evening, all being well.

Their faces were red, puffy and tear-stained. No wonder.

"Mum, Dad – I tried to dig him out. They said he's in hospital. When can I see him? I want to see my husband." They looked at one another in only that way that people who've been married forever can do. They didn't need to speak but something passed between them. In an echo of Breda's actions of the evening before Mum took my hand and gently stroked it.

"Vera. It's not Stan who's in hospital. It's Harry. They say it's touch and go whether he'll ever walk again."

"You mean…?"

"Yes, love," said my father. "It's Stan who was killed. Oh, Vera, we're so sorry."

How could this have happened twice? I broke down in tears and the people in the other beds all looked over at me. I didn't care that I was making a scene. If anyone had the right to scream the place down, I thought I did. I was angry. Angry with Stan for leaving me. Angry that I didn't even have our baby to remember him by. Furious with whatever god there was that could do this to me. The irony. My first love killed abroad in this stupid, stupid war, and the second man, the one I'd married, in a safe occupation – a cushy number back in Blighty – he'd only gone and copped it too. Was there no safe place for the men in my life? Even my brother would spend the next year or more in a specialist hospital unit trying to get back the use of his legs.

I began to believe I was a jinx. Two young men I'd fallen in love with, both in the flush of their youth and strength, and now they were dead. The older brother I'd idolised from my cradle, crippled by an enemy bomb. Would I dare ever to give my heart to another man without feeling that I condemned him to death too?

I wanted to be cold-hearted. I wanted to be the Ice Queen and never care for another person again. I couldn't get over the unfairness of it all but as time moved on, I realised other people were going through similar things. Tiny babies killed in air-raids – mothers getting the dreaded news that two, even three, of their sons had died in this disgusting war. I wasn't alone with my grief. Not truly alone.

6

AS TIME CREPT FORWARD - for it did creep now, for me – I had nothing in my life to live for, or so it felt – we had to pick up the pieces of our lives and move on. Harry was moved to a special unit and we were allowed to visit him once a week. The journey was long and travel difficult so we rarely managed to get there more than once a month. He seemed in good spirits but spent much of his time on his back. He had physiotherapy and hydrotherapy but to me, progress seemed snail-slow. I was used to the active, strong brother I'd grown up with and here was a broken shell of a man with atrophied leg muscles and a brow etched with pain. All I could do for him now was hope, and I felt that my hope had been completely used up.

In the immediate aftermath of the air-raid we

had moved into my Aunt Janet's house but even with my cousins away fighting, we were cramped there. Eventually my parents managed to rent a small cottage in Ayling, just outside of the town, but close enough to be able to travel back in to our jobs every day. I made a rapid recovery from my miscarriage – at least physically. I was young and strong and the doctors kept telling me there was no reason why I wouldn't have many more children. I know they meant it kindly but in the face of losing two men, I didn't know how to tell them that I couldn't or wouldn't have any more. My heart had callused over and I felt I would never love again.

I had to make some progress towards getting back my old life and I began by putting away the dark mourning clothes I'd worn in the aftermath of Frank's death and, again, since Stan was taken from me. The old yellow rain mac and sou'wester came out and I tried to put on the jaunty air I'd had all those years ago. I wasn't that girl. I never again could be but I didn't have to wear navy and grey and accompany them with a long face and downturned mouth. That wouldn't bring my lads back.

I got out my old red coat again too. It was the one Frank had always loved. I'd not worn a coat often over that golden summer of '39 but occasionally I'd toss it in the back of his father's car in case the evening turned chill. He used to turn the collar up around my face and drop a kiss on my nose. Oh, those times will never come again. I wear the yellow more than the red these days. Red still reminds me of blood. Too much blood.

My mother complained that I'd become pale and sickly looking. I went to work and I went to bed and not much happened in between. I'd lost the will and the reason for all those walks on the downs, those evenings outside, sometimes taking exercise, sometimes just lying under the fluffy sky and the waning sun. I couldn't face them alone. I got no fresh air, no exercise, no long relaxation for my eye muscles. I saw this tedious future stretching out like my image in the side mirrors of Grandma's old dressing table – on and on endlessly.

I began to force myself to take a short walk

each day. It was a much more pleasant activity in Ayling than it had been in the town where the derelict areas and empty crofts were a dismal reminder of what we'd all lost. I felt sick when I heard people speak of winning the war. What had I won that was of more value than the things I'd lost?

Nobody wins when so many lose their lives.

In some senses it feels as though the war is still with us. We still have rationing. We've been promised rebuilding but the broken skylines mock us. It hasn't happened yet. We have nothing to feel triumphant about. Nevertheless, I chose my old red coat this morning. I must make some effort to raise my spirits or I'll die an embittered old woman. I bought this red umbrella with the same intentions – to try to recreate the high spirits, the light-heartedness of my pre-war girlhood. I almost bought a black one – as my mother would say, it won't show the dirt – but I still have a little rebellious corner of my soul and it yearns for brightness and light.

Oh, the car is so like his father's. It's drawn up a few yards down the street and sits now, chugging on the glistening cobbles as I fight the wind for possession of my umbrella. He's got out, now, the man who looks so much like my dead love. It must be him. It is him! I pause to look over the railings into the pond, to see my reflection, face even whiter than usual.

I'm going to turn, now. It is going to be him. It is him!

The Watcher

THAT'S YOUNG VERA. Her family moved into the village after they'd been bombed out and her poor husband killed. Terrible business. And what a god-awful day to be out. It's as if the heavens are raging. The rain, the wind. She ought to go back home and dry off.

She's stopped her usual walk and she's looking over the water there. I wonder what she's thinking? She's been still a long time, considering the evil weather. Those clouds are full. It's going to tip water down all day. I don't suppose the ducks mind but even my little dog, always up for a run whatever the weather, is looking rather damp and dispirited. It's only since that man got out of the car that he's bucked up and looked interested. No sticks to throw for you here, Benjie.

They're walking slowly towards one another. I wonder if they knew each other a long time ago. Neither looks convinced.

Ah, now they've recognised each other. They must be old friends for they've just grasped one another in the most fearsome hug. I do hope this is the end of a happy story. I can hear them both saying, 'Is it you? Is it really you?'

Sometimes you just wish the weather would co-operate. It has no sense of a good story. If ever there was a time when the sun should break out, surely this is it.

Also by Jonathan Hill:

Novels

FAG

Novellas

Pride

The Anniversary

The Maureen Series

Maureen goes to Venice

A Letter for Maureen

Maureen and The Big One

Maureen's Christmas Carol

Maureen Gets Crafty

Short Story Collections

Eclectic: Ten Very Different Tales

Beyond Eclectic

100 One Hundred Word Tales

Beyond 100 Drabbles (with Kath Middleton)

Also by Kath Middleton:

Ravenfold

Message in a Bottle

Top Banana

www.jhillwriter.com

www.kathmiddletonbooks.com

Made in the USA
Charleston, SC
28 March 2016